This book is dedicated to those people who don't look back fondly at aspects of their childhood experience.

✽ ✽ ✽

CONTENTS

In The Mobiles

I'm sitting in a sweaty classroom dreaming about my dinner. It's in the middle of a mobile wooden hut divided into three. These classrooms are known as the Mobiles. As I glance at the clock, I feel the teacher following me. I glimpse his lifted arm and realise he's about to fire something in my direction. He executes, and the missile skims my head before catching the ear of the boy behind.

"That was meant for you, McCoubrey, and nobody else but you."
 It is no consolation for Johnny O'Neill, whose ear is bleeding. "You're supposed to watch me, not the bloody clock. I'm the one you're supposed to watch. *M E MEEEE.* Dinner time's when I say so, and none of you will leave the classroom until then. You, McCoubrey, will be last out. So pick that bloomin' duster off the floor and set it back on my desk where it belongs."

I bend to retrieve the duster. Scrabbling at O'Neill's feet, I feel the weight of forty staring classmates. I want to stay on my hunkers, but I can't. The stench from O'Neill's socks makes getting back up compulsory. Dirty blurt! Avoiding eye contact with O'Donnell, I slip back to my seat. I sit calmly for the rest of the morning, outwardly paying attention to today's lesson.

When the clock's big hand clearly shows two minutes past noon, we can leave. O'Donnell has a great smirk on his face. As I trudge out last, he winks at me. It's his way of saying, "That'll teach you." As I stroll away from the mobile, knowing that my dinner's getting cold, I hear myself muttering: "Frig you, O'Donnell, frig you."

I join the last few stragglers fighting their way into the canteen. We finally get a seat right at the back of the third row. Unfortunately, it means that we will be the last pupils served. There are eight pupils at each table. The two pupils at the end of each table collect the food from the dinner ladies. I glance around the hall and notice my two mates at the third table of row two. McGann nudges Crozier. They both nod mockingly at me before diving back into their plates.

I observe them and momentarily feel alone and isolated, sitting in the middle of the last table with guys I don't know or like. I'm about to be served by a fourteen- year old town scruff and a fat farmer's son who hasn't washed for a week. The dinner ladies usually give the servers large portions to reward them for their duties. I picture Bonanza Bill the culchie as a dinner lady, doling out the food behind the canteen hatch. He serves himself spuds, peas, and roast beef, piled high on a bin lid, and I receive a few beans on a cracked saucer.

The food arrives. Sausages, peas, mashed potatoes, and gravy! I usually leave the meat to the end and mix the rest. Any observer would know what I am eating. Now I'm sittin' beside someone who has mashed everything, then added half a bottle of brown sauce. It looks like a lump of shit and starts to smell likewise.

This situation is a massive test because even though I'm starvin', I have a bit of a phobia for such things. My strategy is to rest one elbow on the table and turn the other way. But I can't ignore this situation. So I set my plate to one side and suffer in silence. I stare forlornly at every drooling mouthful. Bits of food fall back onto the plate and are immediately retrieved. He has discarded his knife and fork and uses his spoon as a shovel. In a couple of years, he'll make a good farm labourer. Within sixty seconds, he devours his dinner. He lifts the plate with both hands, like the tennis champion at Wimbledon. Drawing it close to his slobbery face, he licks the gravy mush dry. I stare at him, repulsed, but he doesn't notice a thing. Such misery I endure every day.

Nothing can ever prevent me from eating dessert. When the rice and peaches arrive, I'm relieved there isn't much scope for the farmer's son to make a pig's ear out of it. I swallow the peaches whole and devour the rice. I need to get away as quickly as possible. As I step out from the wooden bench, I vow to avoid the same table in the future. I thank God I'm not one of the other seven boys with whom I have just shared a table. I'm glad that I'm me, McCoubrey.

My name's Barry-Joe McCoubrey There's only one other Barry in our area. It was my ma's choice as she wanted something unusual. Joe was tagged on to make it different. Double-barrelled Christian names are rare, Paddy-Joe Metcalfe and John-Joe Fox being the only ones I've heard of. But as far as I know, I'm the only one in the town called *Barry*-Joe. I like that and also like the fact that I'm known as Barry-Joe and not simply Barry. I don't understand why people have two names if one is immediately redundant. I have a neighbour called Aloysius Raphael Glendenning. Not the best handle to have on your jug! We call him Al. Then there's Benedict Joseph Farrell. Ben!

The McCoubrey bit is more problematic. That's my da's name, so there was no picking and choosing, but unfortunately, I have the same surname as a renowned local TV broadcaster, Harry McCoubrey. Harry is supposed to read the news each evening but always finishes with a little quip or wisecrack. For example, last night, there was a report about "Local Manual Labour." At the end, McCoubrey said: "I always thought that Manual Labour was a Spaniard." He then put on his mischievous grin. When I went to school today, the boys repeated the joke for my benefit. "That's a good 'ne," they said, laughing. "You're a real character McCoubrey, a real bag of fun. How do you do it night after night? Christ, that was a good one last night. Tell it to us again; go on, tell it again." All morning they've kept asking me if it's true that Manual Labour is a Spaniard. I laughed because, to be honest, I think that Harry's joke *was* quite funny.

I'm used to this ritual and learned early on that it is sarcasm. My ma has frequently told me that sarcasm is the lowest form of wit. I either laugh at their jibes or retort with: "Trying to be sarcastic?" Or: "Did you know that sarcasm is the lowest form of wit." When I use this response, I'm conscious that I'm repeating my ma's words. It makes me feel like a bit of a fraud, but it doesn't stop me. In my opinion, Harry McCoubrey *is* quite funny sometimes. At least he's different. I'm secretly pleased to share the same surname. Good old McCoubrey!

After dessert, I drift around the school playground, a square piece of gravel directly adjacent to the canteen. Saint Columba's is a Boys' School for seven to fifteen-year-olds; it is a cold grey stone building, identified by its prison-like perimeter wall. The only escape is via a giant iron gate the same colour as Bonanza Bill's dinner. Pupils aren't part of the outside world until dinner and their home time at three o'clock.

I wander round the side towards the toilets. They're known as the outside toilets, which would be ok if the school had any *inside* ones. It doesn't. Some young boys are playing marbles at the bottom of the school steps. One of them looks like a TV character called the Milky Bar Kid. My money's on him. The stench from the toilets is powerful, and I haven't reached it yet. Upon entering, I see three or four boys from my class chatting beside the dank brown urinal wall. I recognise Michael Mackie, so I know what will happen.

Mackie is the school champion at pissing the highest. The wall is six feet tall, but that doesn't deter Mackie. His record is about five and a half feet. I observe his technique closely, especially as I showered myself in my urine when I last tried to improve his mark. First, he takes his Willie and gives it a few loving strokes. He follows up with a couple of tugs. Then he grabs it and squeezes its head with his thumbs and forefingers. Finally, he points it skywards. A skinny squirt of urine shoots into the air, but a gust of wind persuades it to shower the admiring spectators. "You're taking the piss," one of the boys shouts as Mackie has another go. He shrieks joyously and turns his dangler towards them, spraying what remains in his bladder. They all start laughing. "You were in good form last night, McCoubrey," says Mackie as he brushes past me on his way out. "A Spaniard, eh?" He looks delighted with his little jibe. His mates follow him out, happily rubbing their stains.

God help anyone who has to do more than urinate in these outside toilets. *Everything* is open air. When it rains, your head becomes an umbrella. If you're not swift in applying the tracing paper that passes as toilet roll, you wash your ass instead of drying it. There's no such thing as peaceful contemplation in this place. It's a case of in, trousers down, job done, and out. All performed as speedily as possible because, to be brutally honest, it's shameful being anywhere near these toilets. That's why I've taken up smoking. If I see anyone I know on my way out of the bog, I tell them I've just been for a quick smoke. "That's just what I'm about to do now," they reply. The clever ones tell me to make sure that I wash my hands.

Soon the bell rings. It's the end of the dinner break. I've watched someone eat shit and others drink piss. Is this my life? I trudge back to the Mobile, hoping the next few hours will pass quickly. Suddenly I remember that today is Thursday, 4-a-side football day, depending on O'Donnell's mood. I think of the duster incident, and my spirits dampen. We arrive before him. He's chatting to one of the other Mobile teachers, finishing his cigarette. When he enters, silence reigns, and he surveys the classroom, checking that he has everyone's attention. It means we should be facing him, awaiting instructions.

"Since it's almost the end of term, I thought we'd have some singing practice. O'Donnell is smirking, waiting for a reaction. Someone chirps up.
"Singing, sir?"
"That's right, sonny Jim, like Val Doonican, Perry Como, Jim Reeves, Big Tom and the Mainliners, Charlie Pride."
"Does that mean Country and Western, sir?"
"Smart Alec, eh! Stewart, you've just given me a good idea there.

Let's divide you up - cowboys on my left and townies on my right."

A meek hand goes up.

"Sorry, sir, but I live right on the edge of the countryside," says Damian Doran. "I don't know what that makes me?"

"That makes you a cowboy, Doran. Are ye only realisin' it now?"

The pupils burst into laughter. I smile because I don't think it's *that* funny. Even if it was the most amusing remark in the world, there's no way I'll give O'Donnell the satisfaction of seeing me laugh. The memory of the wooden duster is far too fresh for that. I hate myself for smiling but consider it a wry smile under duress. It wouldn't have helped the four-a-side prospects if I hadn't reacted. I decide there and then that if a future similar situation arises and it's not a football day, I'll sit stony-faced. *The funnier he is, the more deadpan I'll look.*

"Ok, cowboys on my left, townies on my right and Doran in the middle."

The class laughs again, but I know this isn't the stony-faced moment. So we divide into two groups, and I share a desk with Mitch Crozier.

"The song we're going to sing is: **I Know a Girl**. The cowboys will start by singing the first line, **I Know a Girl That You Don't Know**, and the townies will sing the chorus, "**Little Lisa Jane, Little Lisa Jane**.""

He sings the tune.

"Ok. One, two, three."

He points his left index leftwards, and the country boys get stuck into the words.

 "I know a girl that you don't know."

O'Donnell's right index points right.

 "Little Lisa Jane, little Lisa Jane."

It's a bit feeble, but it's an effort.

"Let's go again. Come on now, let's give it some stick."

The cowboys happily respond.

"I know a girl that you don't know."
"Townies"?
We're getting into it now.
"Little Lisa Jane, little Lisa Jane."
"Great. One more time."

We townies are glancing at each other. In our midst is the class prankster and hard man, Joey McGann. His right index finger covers his lips, so we take note. The country boys are already in great voice. "I know a girl that you don't know." The mobiles are vibrating, and O'Donnell is animated. He's the conductor pulling all the strings. Then, as the cowboys reach their crescendo, he flicks his wrist rightwards. "Take it away, townies," it commands. "Take it away."

Silence! A deafening nothingness! O'Donnell swivels round in slow motion, his happiness fading into surprise, then misery. I'm choking with laughter and cough deliberately to stifle it. He'll *break* that duster over my head if he catches me laughing. I compose myself. O'Donnell also calms himself in a very deliberate manner.

"I'm going to give you townies the benefit of the doubt. And I'm going to imagine that you must have forgotten the words because woe betides if I discover something more sinister going on here… if you're starting to play silly buggers with me on a Thursday afternoon, then I'll be the one to finish it off. You can bloody well bet your bottom dollar on that so you can. It takes two to tango, and I can tango with the best of them."

He seems to be enjoying the challenge. Turning to the blackboard, he writes the following words in block capitals. LITTLE LISA JANE, LITTLE LISA JANE. Swinging around, he addresses the cowboys.

"Some of these townies need a bit of help occasionally. That should remind them, and as some of them can't spell, I've even spelt the words for them." He produces one of his menacing smiles. I recognise O'Donnell's mood change because he has just sighed audibly, and his bald head is sweating. Glancing behind, I notice my mate McGann's expressionless face and folded arms. The other townies are shuffling uncomfortably in their seats. I glance at Crozier, but he doesn't flinch.

"A one-two, a one-two-three."

O'Donnell beckons the cowboys to sing. They respond vigorously, digging each word out deliberately.

"I know a girl that you don't know."

They turn automatically to their left, trying to lasso us into action. I'm watching them watching us when I suddenly become engulfed in a screaming chorus.

"LITTLE LISA JANE, LITTLE LISA JANE."

The wooden desks vibrate, and I look behind in time to see McGann bellowing the words as if his life depended on it. Serious concentration covers his face as he chants like a football hooligan. The other townies are smiling as they sing. I'm between a rock and a hard desk. I don't want to appease the teacher, and I don't want to taste that duster. So rice and peaches will do for today! My gob is half open, and as my "comrades" conclude their line, I hear myself murmur, "*Jane*".

I don't *say* the word, though I don't *sing* it either. It's a type of grunt, an involuntary mumble. I want it acknowledged that I'm making an effort. Tagging along, admittedly behind the rest, but still in tow. Although I'm unhappy with the proceedings, that muttered grunt is my contribution. *I'm not like the other townies or the cowboys but like me. I'm McCoubrey, and you can like it or lump it. That goes for the whole friggin' lot of ye.*

"I see you've found your tongues."

 O'Donnell is pacing back and forth across the room. He does this for about a minute, with his head bowed in contemplation. Then, finally, he has a full stretch.

"Aaaggghhhh......what day is today anyway? Thursday? Eh, let me see now. Thursday, Thursday afternoon. Maybe a good day for football?"

The cowboys smile while the townies remain apprehensive. "What do *you* think, McCoubrey...is it a good day for a game of football?"

"It's not too bad, sir, I suppose."

I don't want to seem too keen. A gentle prompt is the best policy. I know that O'Donnell's a volatile character who's testing me. I'm not sure whether he has spied my belated contribution to the class sing-along, but for a man with eyes in the back of his head, there's every chance he has.

"Don't be noisy when you're leaving the room. Other classes are doing proper work," he says deliberately.

An excited stir hisses through the room as the classmates realise they're getting the football. Smiles and hurried chats become the day's order as the atmosphere transforms. Doran isn't bothered about being called a cowboy if it means he can play his favourite game. His buck teeth are on show like the keys of a piano. We start trundling towards the door. I have a phobia about confined crowds, so I linger at my desk on these occasions. When the rush has thinned out, I move towards the exit and join the stragglers.

"Where are *you* going, McCoubrey?" says O'Donnell, guarding the door.

"I was going out to the schoolyard."

"What for?"

"To play football, sir."

"Is that right, sonny Jim... well, I've got a wee surprise in store for you because you won't be playing football this afternoon. Instead, you'll be sitting here on your own, learning the words of that last song by heart so that you'll never forget them again. Is that all right?"

What a thing to ask me! *'Is that all right'?* The bastard knows that I love football, and his words are a slow dagger through my heart. Feeling sickly and emotional, I stare at the ground and nod slightly. The last few pupils disappear along with O'Donnell, and the door bangs shut.

I wander instinctively back to my seat. The feeling of alienation overwhelms me, and I start sobbing. No one is watching as I sprawl my head onto the hard desk and protect it with my joined arms. Now I can cry in peace, and I do. It's a dark place, but I feel strangely safe here. *This is where your stubbornness has got you, McCoubrey. You're missing your beloved football because of it.* I think about my mother's constant warnings about not cutting off my nose to spite my face. Too late, McCoubrey, the damage is done.

The faint shouts of my classmates drift in from the yard. "Over here, come on, pass the ball. Yes! Oh no! What a goal!"

"Frig them, frig them all. Frig the whole world."
I wipe my eyes and pick up my fountain pen and paper. In my best handwriting, I write some words. *I know a girl that you don't know, Little Lisa Jane, Little Lisa Jane.* I start to hum the words. I mutter them. Then I sing them aloud. And again. I alternate between townie and cowboy and think about Doran.
  "That's right, Doran, you're a town cowboy just like me....giddy up there, boy, giddy up, giddy up to fuck."
Now I'm the teacher leadin' the singin'. *"Ok, cowboys, take it away. Come on, hit it. I know a girl that you don't know."* I flick my wrist to the right. *"Townies, let's be havin' ye."*
  "Little Lisa Jane, Little Lisa Jane."
"Yous can do better than that, for Christ's sake. I want ye all to take the roof off this piece of wooden shit.
"I know a girl that you don't know."
"Little Lisa Jane, Little Lisa Jane."
They're unstoppable. I recline in my big teacher's chair and spot a small pupil among the cowboys.
"You call yourself a cowboy O'Donnell, whimpering like that. Look at the cut o' ye. Twelve years old and as baldy as a coot. If I were a baldy bastard like you, I'd wear a cowboy hat to hide it. Have ye no shame

*at all, O'Donnell? Answer me **now,** you nincompoop.*
"No," he whimpers.
"No, what?"
"No, sir."
"That's what I like to hear, O'Donnell."

I lift the duster and pout my lips. He's quivering in his boots, probably shittin' himself.
"If you shit yourself, you're for the outside toilets, O'Donnell. Ok, cowboys and shitty pants, let's be havin' ye one more time."
This is great. To hell with the football. Frig O'Donnell and frig the rest of the class. I stroke my nose. It's still there. I smother my face with my right palm. Intact! Remembering that I'm also a cowboy, I repeat the exercise with my left hand. Still there! *So you all think that McCoubrey is a cowboy? You're damn right he is, and you can bet your bottom dollar on that.*

Home Time

The end of football usually coincides with the end of the school day at three o'clock. Today is no different. As the other boys return from the playground huffing and puffing, I slip away quietly. I have to be quick as my mother has told me to collect my younger sister from the local convent school. I scurry down Carlton Street, turn right into Thomas Street, and see the top of the convent building. Soon I spot the Lollipop man guiding young children across the road. He's one of the most miserable-looking people I've ever seen. His lollipop seems to be a burden rather than a blessing. If it was an actual lollipop, I doubt that he would suck it. I'm sure he would probably let it melt. His sad expression is a permanent facial feature beneath his Lollipop man's cap. I'm sure he wears both of these things to bed.

There's another Lollipop man at the Protestant primary school nearby. He's a quirky old git who loves his job and is meticulous about his duties. Some boys from my school often knock the cap off his head. Joey McGann did it last week, and the old guy went berserk. He threw the stick at McGann, but it missed, hitting a passer-by in the leg. No one would ever consider such a stunt with the convent guy. It would be far too risky. Being twelve would be irrelevant if he identified you as the culprit. Sometimes you know things.

When I reach my sister's classroom, I hear some commotion. I peer through the glass pane at the side of the door. My sister Lona spots me and gestures for me to wait outside. A bespectacled grey-haired nun is addressing one of the pupils, who I recognise as Kevin Darry.
"Try again, Darry. I want you to spell bicycle."
A small red-faced boy in the back row starts to tremble.
"B... I...S... I..C...K."

Some of the other thirty-five pupils are raising their hands at this stage.

"Sister, sister."

Sister Agnes ignores them.

"Darry, do you have a bicycle?"

"Yes, sister."

"Does it work?"

"Yes."

"So it's not sick then."

The children laugh.

"No, sister."

"Try again then."

"BISICK."

Darry clearly hasn't understood the hint. He has a tortured look on his face, like someone who has been given a "mission impossible". For Darry, it *is* impossible to spell bicycle. I can spell it quickly, and when he says *S* for the second time, I find myself mouthing the word *C* through the pane of glass. He notices me and knows that I am trying to rescue him. It only exasperates him further. I make a C shape with my index finger, but he becomes more flushed and confused. Maybe he thinks the shape is the first part of S because he doesn't correct his mistake.

BISICK is Darry's best effort, but it isn't good enough for Sister Agnes.

"Come to the front of the class, Darry. I have a little present for you."

He obeys. The nun prods him under the chin to make him stand upright. Then she produces a green paper hat with the words **DUNCE** written across the front. Most of the class is giggling. A few are pointing. Sister Agnes scrawls **BICYCLE** on the blackboard and points it out to Darry. "That's how to spell bicycle, and that's why you're wearing the dunce's hat."

Tears are streaming down his face. When I look at Lona, she's gaping at Darry. She isn't giggling like the rest of the class, but

I'm sure I caught her smiling a moment ago. He bows his head, searching for solace on the classroom floor. There is none.

"Return to your seat and keep that dunce's hat, Darry. That's your prize for being stupid."

I watch Darry clutch his dunce's hat as if it *is* a prized possession. Maybe he's trying to squeeze the life out of it, as it has done to him. The ground didn't open up and swallow him as he had wished. He only escaped when Sister Agnes eventually released him from his agony. How cruel can one be towards a nine-year-old boy? *That nun is a bitch, and the other children sicken my guts. I despise the lot of them.*

This episode makes me think about my experiences at the same convent school a few years ago. If you did something wrong, the punishment was sharing a desk with a girl for the afternoon. Not *any* girl! In my case, the teacher always chose an ugly one. I would have preferred *six of the best* with her wooden cane as punishment, but I got Doris Blakely or Betty Reed instead. Doris hadn't washed for a fortnight, and Betty had breath that smelled fouler than Bonanza Bill's dinner. She also had her fair share of spots. If I were beside either of them, I'd sit with my elbow on the desk, facing the opposite way. Some things repulse me.

Me and Lona walk in silence to the bus stop. We pass our granda's house, number nine Coronation Street. My granny lives there too, but it's *his* house. She's the housewife. There's a white semi-circle outside the front door, where my granny has scrubbed daily for years. It's so clean that everyone steps over it when they visit. I don't like going there on weekdays. No atmosphere.

"That was friggin' awful; what happened in your class there now. Sister Agnes is a crabbit bitch, so she is."

"I know. It *was* awful," replies Lona. Kevin Darry is the quietest person in the class, so he is. He wouldn't say boo to a goose, so he wouldn't."

Lona is sniffling.

"She picks on somebody different every week, so she does. I'm

dreading that she'll pick on me soon. I'd die, so I would."
She offers me a Love Heart. Because of the commotion over the dunce's hat, we have missed the last school bus. It means that we have two choices. Either take the town service bus or walk. The town service bus is for everyone, not just schoolchildren. It takes the scenic route and is pretty slow, but it's a good alternative if you miss the school bus. We don't have long to wait.

I like to sit quietly when I'm on the town service bus. There's something peaceful about sitting at the window and watching the world outside. The view isn't unique—houses, women with messages in their shopping bags, children, the local football ground, the metal box factory, a few sweetshops, a level crossing and a roundabout. These markers signal that I'm getting closer to home. By observing them, I can escape the chatter inside the bus, usually about the weather or last night's episode of Crossroads. I buy two halves from the conductor and help Lona with her Love Hearts. I love the smooth click of the ticket machine when the conductor spins its chrome handle. Sometimes it doesn't function the first time, so I get a double thrill. If he has to sift through his soft black leather bag for change, I soak in its aroma. I'm a twelve-year-old boy who gets enjoyment from buying a bus ticket. Is that normal?

Two hundred yards from our stop, a big fat man filling two seats demands to be let off the bus. When the conductor tells him to wait until it stops, he stands up slowly. His bulk fills the aisle.
"I live here, so let me off here. It's too far for me to walk back from the next stop," he says to the driver, ignoring the conductor.
"I'm not allowed to stop the bus unless it's at the bus stop," replies the driver.
"No one's going to know except you and me," retorts the massive lump of flesh, a touch menacingly. "I won't tell anybody if you don't."

Another fifty people are on the bus, and we're engrossed in

the drama. His cheek amuses me, and although part of me wants him to get his way, I mostly want to see him humiliated and forced to get off at the regular bus stop, like the rest of us. Why should fat tubs get preferential treatment? Mind you, he *is* abnormally large, so maybe he's got a disease. However, even though this man might have a severe health problem, I'm adamant that he should waddle home from the same location as other passengers and start picturing this scene when the conductor tells the driver: "Just let him off." The bus makes a special stop on Loughgall Road, and we all wait patiently while Billy Bunter manoeuvres off. He faces the bus until it moves. I can't work out whether he's taking a rest or having an on-the-spot lap of honour.

We arrive home minus the Love Hearts. The stop is ten yards from our house. You might think that this is handy. However, catching buses isn't a family trait; at least three times a week, one McCoubrey or another is the last person to scramble aboard. Lona tells our ma about Billy Bunter while I make some milky bread. This is bits of bread boiled in milk and sugar. When it becomes slushy empty it into a bowl or devour it straight from the saucepan if you're starvin'. When I taste the softened, crusty bits, I feel a surge of energy in my bones. Today's dinner time fiasco is soon forgotten. I'm relaxed and alive, home from school at last.

I'm the eldest of three McCoubrey children. We are aged twelve, nine, and seven. My mother, Rosemary, is a housewife, and my father, Danny, is a joiner. She runs the house, and he pays for it. We live in Redville, a housing estate with about three hundred homes. Most of them are pebble-dashed and whitewashed. With only three children, our family is small compared to most other Catholic families in Redville. But my ma's only thirty-two, and Crozier's ma had a child when she was forty. Some of the Catholic families from our estate are very poor, but they have the consolation of an inside toilet. Not everybody in Portstown can make such a boast. Most Protestant families have only two or three children, and the men seem to have decent jobs. Their children wear uniforms to *primary* school. Many of their houses have parked cars outside. We go to different schools, and on Sundays, we go to Mass while they lie in bed until dinner time. Sometimes I'd love to be a Protestant!

My friend Peter Pope asked me recently what it was like to get up at eight o'clock every Sunday morning, and I told him that you get used to it. However, there's nothing to get used to because it has always been like this. The only chance of a lie-in at our house is on Saturdays, but sometimes the coal man comes at seven-thirty, and the rumble of the coal tumbling into the coal shed sounds like a volcano. End of the lie-in!

We have banana sandwiches for tea. My mother puts a big plateful on the table, and we scramble for them. Being the eldest, I win. I don't sit at the table. Instead, I'm attracted by the catchy music of Crossroads, and I plop down on a wooden chair to see what excitement is taking place at the motel. This is my entertainment. I don't *want* to watch Crossroads. It's my mother's favourite programme, but she rarely gets to sit and watch it. Once, I switched channels, and she gave me a good cuff around the ear. "I'm watching Crossroads," she said as she returned to the cooker. She has to cook a proper dinner for my father every night - potatoes, meat and vegetables, and if it's not ready when he arrives home, the atmosphere is hateful.

Someone knocks on the door, and Ben opens it.
 "It's Peter Pope asking if you're in."
"Where else could I be?" I shout from the kitchen. "Tell him I'm watching Crossroads."
I can see him via the hall, but he can't see me. Finally, the door closes, and I feel a bit guilty.
 "Why don't you get up off your backside and get out of my sight for a while?" says my mother.
"I'm eatin' my tea," I reply and return to Crossroads.

I feel uncomfortable for a few minutes. First, there was the dinner business earlier today, and now this. Why does every bloody meal have to be spoiled? I go upstairs, and through the net curtains of the bedroom window, I spot Peter Pope sitting on a garden wall, talking to another boy. Now I don't feel so guilty. There's no way that I'm going out tonight.

Waxwings No More

Friday is my favourite day. I can smell the coming weekend, which sustains me during school hours. Yesterday's duster episode is history, and I arrive unusually early to school. Mitch Crozier and Joey McGann are already there and have a plan. Crozier comes over to me.
 "McCoubrey, have you ever smelled Batten?"
"What for?"
"He must piss himself every night because when he comes in here, he's stinkin'."
"Now that you mention it, I smelled piss from him a few weeks ago."
 McGann butts in.
"Right McCoubrey, when he comes in, drop a threepenny bit near his feet. We'll all pretend to look for it, and we can have a good sniff at the same time."
"He'll know there's something fishy."
"Aye, his friggin' underpants," roars Crozier.

I turn to Boot McConville.
"Here, Boot, lend me threepence just for a minute. I'll give it back to ye. Ye know me."
"Aye, I know you, alright. Here's a penny. Has Batten pissed himself?"
"They reckon he pisses himself every day, so we're goin' to check it out… you might as well have a wee sniff yourself."
Boot giggles.
 "Why don't we just pull the trousers off him… he only wears shorts anyway, and if he's pissed himself, we'll give him a good skelpin' on the ass?"
"A good kick on the ass is more like it," says McGann.

"Here he comes boys, here he comes," cries Boot. "Have you got the money, McCoubrey?"

Batten strides into the classroom. I flick the money into the air, and we all scramble for it at Batten's feet. He looks down at us.
"What are yous doin' boys?"
I tell him we're fightin' over a penny and that he can stay there and referee. He looks bemused but stays put. We sniff softly at first and then with greater gusto.
"Shit, there's a bad smell here," cries McGann as he sniffs furiously. "Can you smell anything, Batten?"
"What like?"
"Like friggin' piss."

McGann stands up, clutching the coin, and waltzes back to his seat, putting Boot's penny in his pocket. Boot's laughing because he's also had a good sniff. He knows that he won't be getting his penny back. I have one final snort and am hit by a waft of stale urine. Batten's underpants must be soakin'. I know what it's like to piss myself in bed, but I can change out of the wet stuff in the morning if necessary. Maybe Batten has only one pair of underpants, or he's not wearing *any*. He should do what I sometimes do – remove the underpants and stick a towel between my legs last thing at night, and if the worst happens, the mattress will still be dry in the morning. If he does this, he'll always have a clean pair to put on daily. His only problem will be what to do with the towel. I feel a bit sorry for Batten, but by Christ, what a terrible smell!

We flee to our seats. Batten remains where he is, looking quizzical and blushing slightly. Eventually, he says: "Yous boys are crackers," and heads for his desk. On the way, he catches Boot sniffing and pushes him away. "Your head's cut," he mutters. I interpret this timid reaction as proof that he *has* pissed himself. You'd expect something more aggressive if it wasn't true, like a kick in the ribs. Boot is laughing heartily. He covers his mouth with the side of his hand and turns to the pupil behind.

"Batten's pissed himself."

Johnny Four Eyes doesn't laugh. Instead, he smiles and returns to reading the Dandy.

Enter O'Donnell. He wags his finger at me and beckons me to his desk. He produces a brown ten-bob note. So now I know I'm back in his good books.

"Twenty Embassy and a box of matches, and don't take all day."

I shoot out the door, feeling good. Today isn't wooden duster day for me. Maybe it is for someone else, but it looks like I'm elected. I take the shortcut at the back of the school. It's a back garden that has been unkempt for years. I brush wild bushes aside and follow a well-trodden dirt track that exits at the chapel's side. I see a few religious regulars coming out from the 8.30 Mass. One is wearing a brown headscarf. I've seen her before, and she wears the thing morning, noon and night. She probably wears it to bed. The other is an ancient guy who must be the eldest man in Portstown. His remaining hair is silver, and his eyes are red and watery. He looks like he's preparing for death. I stare at him and *know* that heaven beckons (for him, not me). I'm sure his name isn't Lazareth, but it should be.

Chapel Street is awake as the early shoppers drift into town. A woman with an empty nylon shopping bag walks past, and I wish *I* could go where I pleased. I check and caress the ten bob note. It could buy me fish and chips in Malocco's, with fresh orange juice and a straw. Or I could go down to Woolworths for some broken biscuits. It's early morning, so there's bound to be some left. I could have fish and chips *and* broken biscuits. *Whole* biscuits if I wanted. I calculate that I would still have enough money left for a quarter of Midget Gems, a penny chew and four Blackjacks.

I give O'Donnell his cigarettes and change. No tip! It isn't because he's tight. I'll have to do him one or two more favours before there's any joy. The duster episode is too recent for the giving of tips. Still, I've got a few brownie points in the bag for later.

He tells us to write a paragraph titled: "What Summertime means to me."

It would be easy to claim that summertime is great because there isn't any school for most of it. The first few days off will be great, but attending school will be a blessing in six weeks. So what is there in Portstown that can give real meaning to summertime? It rains all the time, and when it's dry, the drums of the Orangemen rain down instead. The days are long and tedious, and the football season is almost over. Watching cricket is like watching paint dry, but not as good. For me, summer is merely the season that comes before autumn.

I reread the paragraph and know I'm being dishonest. A bit contrary! Summer *is* usually a bit boring, but this year I'm going on my first holiday, and I start secondary school in September. But I don't change a word.

"Shssssssssssss."

It is O'Donnell looking starry-eyed, his index finger tight against his lips. He starts to whisper.

"Not a word, not a word."

He's the only one talkin'.

"I don't want to hear a pin drop…. I've been waiting for this moment for the last twelve months, and it looks like my prayers have been answered; holy be to God."

We're all ears.

"It's the Waxwing. It has returned."

We follow his gaze, and sure enough, a strikingly colourful bird rests on the branch of the pear tree outside. If O'Donnell says it's a Waxwing, then it's a Waxwing. Soon another one lands on the same pear tree branch. Two beautiful Waxwings perched on a pear tree. They ooze class compared to the other scrawny birds on the same tree. If those had any humility, they would find another tree, another town.

"Aren't they stunning?" says O'Donnell.

No one answers because we're afraid to talk. I look round, and

Joey McGann is pickin' his nose and trying to finish his writing. It seems like his immediate priority is his nose because he has just put his pen down and is examining the catch from his right nostril. I hope that he doesn't decide to eat it. O'Donnell glides over to his table and chair.

"I'm going to get my camera," he whispers.

His mouth is open like an alligator. He gently slides his camera from the table drawer, checks it carefully and creeps into position. Facing the window and ready to click, he cranes his neck towards the expectant pupils. Looking chuffed, he winks at the class and whispers: "This one's for posterity."

An almighty fart thunders across the mobile. It rips through the silence, bounces off the back wall and boomerangs around the room before squeaking to a standstill at its starting point. It's from Mitch Crozier's ass. I know because we're sharing the same desk. This one has substance, and a Sumo Wrestler couldn't have mustered up a better effort if he tried. There's too much power and volume for it to have been an accident. Crozier meant it.

We can't help ourselves. Spontaneous laughter erupts. It gets louder and more ridiculous as it cascades through the classroom. Boot McConville is hanging out the side of his desk, and I catch him sneakily sniffing the unsuspecting Batten. Crozier, the culprit, is grinning from ear to ear, valiantly masking his indiscretion. Even the class pansies are amused. I smother my face with my hands so that O'Donnell can't see or hear me. I've heard my da let rip with a few, but I swear to God I've never heard the likes of this. I peep through my fingers and see a pear tree full of shit-coloured scrawny birds. Waxwings no more!

I'm gasping for normal breath, but bits of laughter keep emerging like an endless rope. Simultaneously, I realise I liked those Waxwings' elegance and beauty. From what exotic place did they come? Where will they go? For a fleeting moment, they brought a touch of glamour and mystique to this hateful place, not just the school but Portstown. It was something different, even magical. I even like the name. *WAXWING!* Compare this to Blue Tit, Thrush, Sparrow or Pigeon. No comparison! Waxwing *sounds* like a bird. My thoughts are with the departed Waxwings. Then I relive Crozier's fart and retreat into the palms of my hand. Wherever they're going next, he's given them a flying start. That's for sure.

"That paragraph you were all doing a while ago, I want you to make it into a composition starting now."
The class has become still and attentive. I observe O'Donnell putting the camera back into the table drawer and closing it slowly. His eyes are moist, and I feel uncomfortable. The slapping cane remains untouched. It also looks like Crozier has been spared the wooden duster treatment. Of course, he could always argue that it was an accident. That it just slipped out without asking permission. Or he could try to apologize. *I'm sorry for having farted, sir, and I promise not to do it again.* However, this sounds too much like a church confession, and as far as I know, farting isn't a sin.
I'm sorry about the Waxwings, sir.
This way, he could display remorse that the birds have flown away without taking the blame. I glance at Crozier and see he's busy with his composition. O'Donnell's eyes are almost as red as Lazareth's. I wonder if *he'll* go to Heaven, and I quickly decide there'll be a spell of Purgatory first.

The rest of the morning passes peacefully. O'Donnell doesn't say another word, and Crozier keeps his wind in its pooch. Finally, at midday, O'Donnell opens the Mobile door and signals with his thumb that we are to leave. He might as well tell us to get out of here and not to come back. Ever! We walk silently down the path towards the door that leads into the schoolyard. A crescendo of noise, chatter and uncontrolled laughter breaks the calm of the empty yard.
 "Did you hear that fart of Crozier's?" shouts McGann.

"Hear it? It almost blew me out of the desk."

"Did you see O'Donnell's face? I thought he was goin' to cry. Imagine cryin' over a friggin' Pigeon."

"It wasn't a Pigeon. It was a Waxwing."

"It's all the friggin' same, isn't it? How do you know what it was? Sure, you don't even know your ass from your elbow. I bet those Pigeons, sorry *Waxwings*, are halfway to England by now. They're probably saying to each other: "What to fuck were we doing in a shithole like that anyway."

"Catch yourself on. Don't be daft. Waxwings can't talk, you eejit."

"How do you know? Are you a friggin' bird?"

"You must admit now… they did look nice and colourful."

"Colourful, my ass. Hurry up, or the dinner will be cold."

Our class is first out, so we arrive early at the canteen. McGann and I rush for the top table in row one. It's a tussle, but we get the two outside seats. It means that we'll be serving all the favourites. This table is reserved for solicitors' sons, teachers' sons, teachers' sucks and the son of one of the dinner ladies. There are about five or six of them, so there are usually two or three free places. About fifty boys fight over these. Mind you, there isn't any cast iron guarantee that you'll get a big dinner or dessert just because you serve the Sucks. Ultimately it comes down to the dinner ladies and especially Mrs Lafferty. She's the governor.

Friday is fish day because Catholics aren't supposed to eat meat on Fridays. Nobody has ever told me why. Maybe it's because I've never asked. I used to presume that the authorities that make the school dinners have a rota system and that Friday is fish day. So it never occurred to me that Peter Pope in the Protestant Heart Memorial School is getting tucked into sausages when I am gobbling my fish. Not that I would be too jealous. If it's the nice soft fish with crispy brown batter, that's great. The batter tastes even better than the fish. But that oily fish with all the bones - the one that's supposed to be healthy- it's far too smelly and awkward to eat. They say it's good for you, but choking to death isn't a good way of living. So I usually spit it back onto the plate after getting a bone stuck in my throat.

Today's fish has batter. Me and McGann listen to the fastest "Grace before Meals" I've ever heard. Tommy Lappin, the teacher who has said the prayer, looks as scrawny as those other birds on the pear tree. He should find another school canteen. We charge up to the food hatch. Two plates for McGann, two for me. Two for McGann. Crunch time! The last two dinners will be for McGann and me. The standard line for all servers in this situation is to shout *This Is My Last, Mrs Lafferty*. The hope is that you'll get a bit extra for being the server. Some of the country boys roar these words, even when a different dinner lady is serving.

The women working behind the hatch have a bit of discretion over the size of the portions, but Mrs Lafferty keeps a watchful eye on them. They get a good rollicking if she disapproves of their generosity. It's all right to be stingy. Mrs Lafferty doesn't complain about *that*. Sometimes *she'll* ask the server if this is his last. Of course, Lafferty will have done a mental count beforehand and is nearly always right. If he says *yes,* he'll get a good helping if she likes the look of him. I don't like Mrs Lafferty, and I don't like having to say, "*This Is My Last Mrs Lafferty*." I've tried it several times, and it doesn't work. I've tried it without using her name, a simple *This Is My Last,* but she glares at me as if I'm being disrespectful. The benefit of sitting at the Sucks' table is that everyone *usually* gets a good helping, and it looks like the pupils are getting equal treatment. So for most servers at the Sucks' table, there isn't any need to say *This Is My Last*. But people like me, McGann and Crozier, can't afford to say nothing. I don't know whether it's the way we look, the way we dress or where we live. I don't know if it's the family name. All I know is that I'm starvin', and so is McGann.

This Is My Last. Mrs Lafferty is standing behind the hatch, potato scoop in hand. One scoop, two scoops. She sinks the spoon into the large tin tray of mash for the third time, addressing me gruffly. "This is your last what?" I eyeball her wrinkled old face and her false teeth. Imagine havin' that for a granny. I know what she wants, but she's not gettin' it.

"This is my last visit to the hatch because I've only two more plates to collect."

"Are you trying to be a smart Alec?"

"I'm smart, but I'm not Alec."

"You *are* trying to be smart, aren't you?"

She throws the scoop back into the tray and shoves two plates at me, both containing normal portions.

"Hurry up, away from the hatch now."

"I'll take my friggin' time," I say. And I do.

Me and McGann reverse roles for dessert, so it's his turn to collect the last two plates.

 "Don't say anything to the bitch, McGann."

I can see her eyeing me from the hatch. McGann doesn't speak, but she gives him two ladles of custard and two cakes, twice what she puts onto the other plate! When he returns, he shrugs his shoulders and offers me half of the extra portion. I decline, partly because Lafferty is watching me like a hawk and partly because I have a phobia about eating food from another person's plate. Sometimes I don't mind it if the food hasn't been touched. But I still haven't got over the Bonanza Bill business and don't think I ever will. One nil to the dinner lady, but I swear to God, *this is definitely my last Mrs Ugly, Fucking Granny Bitch, Lafferty.* I'm fucked if I'm going to humiliate myself in front of her again.

On my way out of the canteen, I catch the eye of a pupil from another class.

"Can you see enough," he shouts.

"What are you talkin' about?" I say.

"I said can you friggin' see enough?"

 "Well, I can't see very much from where I'm lookin'."

He marches straight at me, and I know there's no way out of this one. He grabs me around the neck, and I do the same to him. His grip is tighter, and soon I'm pinned to the ground. Finally, he sits on me and asks if I will submit.

"Go and fuck yourself."

He bounces on top of my skinny arms.

"Do you friggin' submit?"

Christ, he's heavy. Mrs Lafferty must have liked him! I look up at the circular throng of excited boys.

"Knock his head in Tam. Go ahead, kick the shit out of him."

I try to struggle free, but I feel clamped. I'm panting heavily, losing my breath. It is a new experience for me. Not the fighting, but getting beat. I prefer to stand toe to toe and use my speed. For about ten seconds, I'm pretty useful this way and speed triumphs over strength. After ten seconds, it gets dodgy, so I have to be wicked and vicious from the first punch. I usually attack with a boot and a fist and score a hit with one of them. From then on, I have the advantage and ram it home. Fist and boot, boot and fist. I use the boot if the other guy is on the floor. I never try to head-butt anybody. I haven't learned how to, and I'm afraid of missing and doing myself more harm than good. I'm a good ball header, but it's not the same.

The only person who head butts in our school is Hector McCurdy. He's got a massive head, so he can't miss. Funnily enough, he can't play football. He prefers to fight. I'm no good at this wrestling business and am not too fond of the stony hardness digging into the back of my skull. Apart from this and the agony in my arms, I'm not taking too much punishment.

"This is your last chance. Do you friggin' submit?"

I want to get up and away from the spectators, gathered like flies around shite.

"Yeah."

It's a whimper, but he heard it. I get up in unison with my conqueror and walk randomly, glimpsing Tommy Lappin emerging from the canteen, massaging his satisfied gut.

He wasn't even older than me, so I can't use that excuse. Apart from my sore arms, I feel fine now. I felt helpless on that hard ground. If that bitch Mrs Lafferty had given me that extra spud and the same dessert as McGann, maybe I could have defended myself better. I try this reasoning with McGann.
"Hard lines McCoubrey. You lost, and that's all there is to it."
He's right.

Returning to class, we see a man in a black suit and white collar talking to O'Donnell. It's Father Quinlan, one of the parish priests. He terrifies the congregation every Sunday at the last mass. This is goin' to be fun. The silence that ruled before lunch retakes charge. We all sit down to wait and watch. O'Donnell is showing Quinlan his camera and whispering something in his ear. It must be about Crozier's fart. The priest stares attentively at O'Donnell, constantly nodding and holding his right ear as if he's about to scratch it.

Nothing will happen until O'Donnell has had his say. He stops talking and looks deliberately around the class. I notice a slight pause when his eyes meet mine. His stare isn't unfriendly. Is he appealing to the decent part of me instead of the stubborn, rebellious, cheeky, cocky bit? I'm unsure, but I wish he would move on to Crozier or McGann. The worst bit is that the priest is also eyeballing us, in sequence with O'Donnell. As well as staring at specific pupils, he snatches steely glances at others. The priest is a big man with a significant presence, and the Sunday congregation will testify that he has a big mouth.

Quinlan gives his right ear a long tug. Then, he starts talking without asking for permission.
"I want to tell you all about the need for prayers in our lives. Prayer is a wonderful thing, you know. God listens, and if he can, he answers our prayers. So what does that mean?"
He pauses and stares around the class. I don't know whether

he's making a statement or asking a question. "What does that mean to *you*?" he mouths. His bulging eyes are glaring in my direction, and I'm trying to work out whether "*you*" means *me* or if he's addressing everybody. I'm not the only one in this class, ye know! What about Batten, Jonny Four Eyes, Crozier, Danny Brown, or the bloody solicitor's son in the front row beside him?

I suddenly recall a conversation with my mother last year when she told me we'd live on homemade pancakes for the rest of the week. This was on a Monday. It hadn't disappointed me too much because I love homemade pancakes, milky bread and banana sandwiches. I remember giving her my concerned face anyway and asking her why. She said that she had no money left. "What are we going to do?" I'd asked.

"Oh, I suppose we'll just have to get by on a wing and a prayer," she'd replied.

I know what Quinlan is doing. He's on about prayers now, but this is all leadin' up to those friggin' Waxwings. The two must go hand in hand, the wings and the prayers. The priest is casting up about the Waxwings. If Crozier farted again, I wonder if they'd come back. They'd hear him all right, but England is far away. I take a chance.

"Father, I think it means that we should all have faith in God so that if we pray, then God will listen very carefully and sympathetically to what we say, but that we shouldn't just pray when we want something. Instead, we should pray because we *want* to talk to God."

It's a brilliant answer, and I know I'm about to be praised. The priest stares admiringly, allowing a lingering pause so the class can digest it.

"Perfect son, perfect. We are all sinners and shouldn't be praying to God just because we want something. We should be praying for the forgiveness of our sins. We are all sinners, *you* and me."

He continues to stare at me. How come I'm always the focus of attention? I hope those cowboys realise that he's talkin' about *them* as well.

"There are many different types of sin. There are mortal sins and?"

"Venial sins, Father."

It's McGann, amusing himself.

"That's right, son: venial sins, venial sins. Now, boys, there are many types of venial sin; one is being rude in class and, yes, being *very* rude when the teacher is trying to point out something wonderful, a gift from God. But we shouldn't mock nature because God created nature in his own light. God created the birds and the bees...the *birds* and the bees."

I knew we'd get there sometime soon. So why doesn't he tell Crozier that farting in class is a venial sin and be done with it?

"If anyone here has committed a venial sin today, he must confess it at his next confession. Is that clear?"

We all nod, and when I watch Crozier, he's nodding like billio.

The priest is a busy man. He cleans his National Health Service glasses, has a few final whispered words with O'Donnell, and leaves. We stand up.

"Good afternoon, Father."

The idiot beside me says: "Good morning Father," and corrects himself. O'Donnell seems to be rejuvenated. When the priest has gone, he says:

"I hope that's given some of you food for thought."

Then we resume with arithmetic.

"For those of you who can't *do* arithmetic, you can at least learn how to spell it?"

I know what's coming because he's covered this one about half a dozen times during the past few years.

A RED INDIAN THOUGHT HE MIGHT EAT TOBACCO IN CHURCH.

"Just remember the first letter of each word, and you're elected."

He's beaming like it's the first time we've heard this. As it happens, I like this sentence and use it to teach my younger brother and sister the same thing. I try to work something out for "Bicycle" but get stuck after "*bring into chapel your.*" It's a pity O'Donnell doesn't teach Kevin Darry from Lona's class.

Drinks Machine

The rest of the afternoon skips by. Me, McGann, and Crozier start wandering.

"A RED INDIAN THOUGHT HE MIGHT EAT TOBACCO IN CHURCH. What do you think about that, boys?"

I'm trying to get the weekend spirit going.

"What's wrong with *Chapel*? *D*oes that mean he's a *Protestant* Red Indian?" says Crozier.

"What's the friggin' difference between a Chapel and a Church, anyway?"

McGann isn't expecting an answer; if he is, I don't friggin' know it.

Crozier isn't listening. He's reading the racing page of the Daily Mirror, which he's just picked up from the footpath. McGann lives in this direction. Sometimes we walk part of the way with him; before we know it, we're outside his front door. "Thanks for walking me home," he'll say, leaving us stranded. Sometimes he'll get a ball, and we'll have a kick about with a few Protestant lads, but I only feel comfortable playing with Protestants from my street. We pass by Jimmy Brownley's and eat the smell of the newly baked soda bread. Last year McGann's aunty gave each of us a slice of Brownley's soda bread, and it was so satisfying that I regurgitated it for the next two hours.

At the corner of Cecil Street, we all stop spontaneously and check to see if we have three-penny bits. I've got one for my bus fare, and Crozier has a tanner. McGann is skint. He knew that before he checked.

"I don't have a penny, boys."

I ask him what happened to Boot's penny, and he says he bought a penny chew from someone at dinnertime.

"I'll change this tanner for two three-penny bits," says Crozier.

He pops into Brownley's and returns with two coins, tossing one for McGann to catch. It hits him on the chest, but he traps it by folding his arms. He peers down and carefully lets the three-penny bit fall into his right hand. Now we know exactly where we're going.

Irish Road Motors is located halfway down Cecil Street. When I first discovered this, I checked all the surrounding street names for any sign of Irish Road. No joy! I thought that it must just be one of those Irish things. Eventually, I found an *Irish Street* half a mile away in the Tunnel. The street didn't have any cars, let alone a garage factory.

We enter the large garage shed a bit sheepishly. We're underage and shouldn't be here. A few short steps and we are facing the large industrial drinks machine. Crozier goes first. He carefully reads the instructions and turns the dial clockwise until the arrow points precisely under the sign: W*hipped Hot Chocolate*. He lets his three-penny bit drop gently into the coin slot. We hear a click, and the device whirrs into action after a tense pause. A plastic cup drops and fills with a frothy, bubbly dark brown liquid. Success! The drinks machine is working. I'm glad Crozier went first. He has his first sip as he steps back and lets McGann get in closer. McGann studies the dial but doesn't adjust it. He slides his three-penny bit into the slot. Nothing happens. He quickly checks the unused coins compartment underneath. His threepence is there. He blows heavily.
"Here, let me do it," says Crozier.
"No, I'll do it myself."

He lets the coin enter more gently this time. The machine clicks, and his face lights up. He takes his first gulp. Now it's my turn. I check the dial—the brown triangular arrow points at the words that say *whipped hot chocolate*. I check again. As I fumble for my three-penny bit, I stare at the arrow. Then I raise the money to the coin slot. One more look! Everything's in order. I follow the example of Crozier and let the three-penny bit drop into the slot. Nothing happens. I scramble frantically at the *returned coins* area. It's there. I need a bit more push, but not too much. My sense of touch is good, so I know the exact amount of pressure to apply when inserting my coin (*you thought you knew the first time McCoubrey*). Deep breath! I free the threepence from my sweaty grip, place it in the slot and push it softly forward. I can hear the click that confirms its acceptance by the machine.

As I step back to enjoy my whipped chocolate making its way to the top of its plastic container, McGann dives forward and twists the dial clockwise. I react instantaneously, desperately flipping it back anti-clockwise. Finally, I get the arrow more or less under the W*hipped Hot Chocolate* sign. I can hear a gurgling inside the machine, indicating that it has made an irreversible choice of drink. I can only step back and wait in trepidation.

A black, strong-smelling, bubbling liquid comes into view and floats quickly upwards until the plastic cup is full. I observe it forlornly. McGann and Crozier are roaring with joy. I smell this stuff. It's coffee, *black* coffee. I check to see where McGann had moved the arrow. *Black Coffee without Sugar!* I'm in shock. A tiny tin of Nescafe lasts for three months in our house. We prefer Rosy Lee. There's no such thing as drinking coffee without sugar. I'm distraught, too wrapped up in my misery to be affected by the laughter of the other two friggers. That was my bus money, my last threepence. I've handed myself a one-and-a-half-mile walk home for *black coffee without bloody sugar*. Since I've paid for it, I'll have to try it. I take a sip and swallow. Horrible! Another sip! Horrible again! I take a final slurp to get my money's worth. Lurching forward, I throw the rest at McGann.

"It's all over the head of you that I've got friggin' coffee instead of hot chocolate."
It splatters at his feet. A little bit spills onto the back of my hand and burns it.
"Friggin' coffee, without friggin' sugar."

When they hear the mention of *no sugar*, their laughter

becomes unstoppable. Finally, I throw the empty plastic cup to the ground, leave them falling about the place, and set off on my long walk home. I walk quickly to get as far away as possible from McGann and Crozier. I don't want to make up and pretend everything's okay with no hard feelings and all that shit. Everything's not okay. It is one of the most heartbreaking moments in my life. That whipped hot chocolate is unique. It's better than any drink, better than any bite of food. I imagine all those little air beads at the top of the cup, puncturing the light, frothy milk chocolate and inviting my mouth to take a good gulp. I take an imaginary sip, but it doesn't taste the same. I'm choking for a drink but a long way from home and penniless.

You're a real frigger, McGann, and you too, Crozier, for laughing. Frig, frig, friggers. I know a girl that you don't know, fuckin' friggers.

I walk pensively through a bus station called the Fair Green. Some Portstown ignoramuses think it's called the "Fare" green because the bus station is here, but it's got nothing to do with bus fares. It's *Fair* Green, not Fare Green! These dopes should put their dunce's hat on, and Sister Agnes can make special ones for them. I'd have a good snigger at the lot of them and wouldn't feel guilty. Why should *I* feel guilty? I'm the one who didn't get the hot chocolate.

It has started to rain. Bucketing down, but I couldn't care less. I can see some people in the bus shelter. I hope they have a long wait. It's a pity there's a bus shelter because I'd prefer it if they got soaked while waiting. A good bloody soaking! Even the housewives! *Especially the housewives,* pregnant or not! If I can't get my hot chocolate, I don't see why they should get their bus. How would *they* feel if they suddenly had to cycle home? If there was a little dial that said B*us,* I could switch it to B*icycle* at the last second and say: "That chucked ye, didn't it?" Or better still, I could have *Bicycle without Chain.* Slap it up them!

As I pass a workshop, I notice a sign saying *Job Vacancies, Apply Inside.* Underneath, there's some more writing in brackets (*NO*

CATHOLICS). I stare at the sign and keep reading it, transfixed. A man is standing on the steps of the workshop entrance. He's smoking, so I presume that he's just a passerby. *I'm* a Catholic. Does that mean that if I wanted to apply for a job here, I couldn't? I wish I were sixteen or seventeen to find out why I can't apply for a job here. Of course, I wouldn't want to work in this shit hole anyway, but that's not the point. Just because I don't like Quinlan doesn't mean I'm a bad Catholic *(it doesn't mean you're a good one, McCoubrey)*. It's my religion that's bein' offended here. If you insult my faith, then you insult me.

I look around to see if I recognise any older Catholic men from Redville, but the area is deserted. There's only me, the smoker and the rain. I glare towards the first-floor offices, hoping to attract the owner's or manager's attention. I maintain my "disgusted" look in case I do. I'm pretty good with these scornful looks and am in the mood to stare scornfully at everyone and anyone.

No one notices me, not even the smoker. He's examining his cigarette butt quizzically like he can't understand why his fag has disappeared. You smoked it, you latchico! I take a last look at the sign and walk on, shaking my head continuously in case the manager is secretly peeping through the Venetian blinds. Portstown people are good at that.

Walking along East Street, I notice some red, white, and blue bunting attached to a few shops. Several houses are flying the Union Jack flag in preparation for the twelfth of July. I wonder if any occupants need a job because some are going in the Fair Green. Maybe I should knock on their door and tell them. Most of them probably have jobs already. Perhaps they could do shift work- their own job in the day and the Fair Green one at night. I look down at my dark shorts and scuffed shoes. I've had these things for about eighteen months, and it's starting to show. But I don't look any scruffier than most other boys my age. At least the ones that go to St. Columba's.

Admittedly Peter Pope does look a bit cleaner and tidier. Is that because he's a Protestant whose family has more money than ours, or he's more hygienic than me? Pope's one of those people who can play with me in the muck and dirt for hours and go home looking squeaky clean while I look like Oliver Twist. He's the son of a Presbyterian. Maybe Presbyterians are immaculate people but come to think of it, Catholics *do* look a lot dirtier than Protestants. Catholic girls have cuts and bruises all over their legs, while Protestant girls have clean creamy skin. They also have better-shaped legs that look elegant instead of bandy and scabby. I remember my Aunt Ita saying to my mother that the difference between the Catholic and Protestant working class was the same as between a penny and a penny half-penny.

"Maybe you're right," said my mother, "but just remember that's fifty per cent you're talkin' about there."

"I never thought about it like that," said my aunty.

My mother always likes to get the last word.

"You see," she said.

I wonder if Protestants use fifty per cent more soap when they wash. I didn't tell my ma this, but a couple of months ago, when I was waiting on the town service bus with Lona and Ben, I overheard one of the Protestant neighbours say to another Protestant neighbour: "She keeps them nice and clean, so she does." Since we were the only children at the bus stop, I knew she was referring to us. I was tempted to say something but liked the woman who commented. She was well-groomed and respectable. It wouldn't have been right to tell her to mind her own friggin' business. If I had used the word "Fuck" on this occasion, my ma would have forgiven me. The other reason I didn't say anything was that I *liked* being perceived as clean and coming from a family that washed their faces and brushed their teeth each morning (*most mornings*)!

I wish that I had a penny or a penny halfpenny now. It's hateful having to pass shop windows full of sweets or to watch other people stuffing their gobs in the street. I dream about Milky Bread, which spurs me to trot until I reach Hetty's, the fruit and vegetable shop. Glancing inside, I see a box of green apples, a sack of spuds, one cabbage, an almost empty onion sack, and hundreds of small brown paper bags. The shop always looks as though it's about to close down. Sometimes it *does* close down for a few days. I don't know why they call it a fruit and vegetable shop. Fruit *or* vegetable is more like it.

I notice the wheelchair man from my street, about twenty yards in front. He's easily recognised as he wears the same Tartan cap and black overcoat daily. People say that he fought in the First World War. He pushes the wheels with his arms until he can get suckers like me to do it for him. Sometimes I don't mind. It's my good deed for the day, making me feel like a decent person. He always lets out a yelp when he wants a push. I get closer and can hear him gasping and panting. He plays up a bit when he spies someone coming his way.

I dwell on the Hot Chocolate again. There's a man a few steps behind me, and I'm sure *he* hasn't experienced what I have today. So I sneak across to the opposite side of the road and rub the side of my face so the wheelchair man won't recognise me. Then, to make doubly sure, I start trotting. When I have reached a safe distance, I peep over my shoulder and see that the wheelchair is trailing behind the walking man. The latter is marching along as if he's afraid his dinner's getting cold. It looks like the wheelchair has come to a complete standstill. "What a selfish git," I think. "How inconsiderate can you get? More worried about your dinner than the cripple." I think I've just heard a yelp. Should I go back and give the wheelchair man a push or not? I slow down and hesitate. Maybe he didn't fight in the war. He could've been born with Polio. I waver but don't have the heart to help.

Booby Prize

There's something about Fridays that can fix everything. When I arrive home, my mother is in the process of unloading her shopping bags. I help her until I see the Paris buns. "Can I have one of these?" I ask her. "Yous can have a half each," she says. My younger brother Ben is watching eagerly. I break the Paris bun in two and give him the smaller half after I've taken a big bite of it. "You're a greedy pig," he shouts, storming out of the kitchen with his bit of bun. I have a fetish about names and recently realised it is a Paris bun, not a *Pars* bun. *Pars* is how we pronounce it in our house. It still tastes the same, of course, but I like pointing out to people that it's a *Paris* bun, a French bun they're eating. I start to explain this to my mother.

"Do you know that this is a French bun?"
"What are you talkin' about?"
"This is called a Paris bun, not a Pars bun. It's from France."
 "Catch yourself on Barry-Joe. It's from the home bakery up the town. That's where it's from."
"But it's originally from Paris, the capital of France."
"Either you're going to eat the bloody thing or not."
"I am, but it's still from Paris."
"Will you give my head peace?"

My sister Lona has been listening to the discussion.
"Will you have a titter o' wit," she shouts. "Who cares if it's a Paris bun or a Pars bun? It's still a bun, isn't it? You can still eat it, can't you? Are you telling me they make those buns in Paris and then bring them all the way to Portstown? Where is Paris anyway, mammy?"
Mammy tells her that it's in another country. She's busy making my da's dinner and doesn't want to prolong the conversation. "Here, Lona, stir that soup will ye," she says. That's her way of

finishing with the subject of Paris buns.

There's a knock at the door. It's the milkman. I know it's him because I can hear his electric milk float outside. He almost takes the door off its hinges with his loud knock. Bang, bang, bang, bang, and when you shout out through the hallway that you're coming, he gives it two more knocks. As it's Friday, he wears a suit because he's not delivering milk and is just collecting the money owed. He looks like he might be going to the bingo hall later. I wonder if he'll go in his milk float. His bill is always exactly right. I bet *he* knows how to spell arithmetic!
"Fourteen bottles of milk and two bottles of orange," he says. "That'll be twelve and six, Mrs."

He knows fine rightly that our second name is McCoubrey, but he likes to call most Catholic wives simply *Mrs.* I've often heard him refer to Protestant Mrs Pope as Mrs Pope and Protestant Mrs Trimble as Mrs Trimble. But he calls my ma "Mrs", Mrs Trucker "Mrs", Mrs Donnelly "Mrs" and Mrs Reynolds "Mrs". The only exception on the Catholic side is Mrs Smith. He doesn't call her *anything*. Bang, bang, bang, bang, and when she answers, he hands her a small piece of paper with the bill written on it. She pays him the exact amount in change without a word. There are rumours that he once had a big bust-up with Mrs Smith's husband. I asked my ma about it one day, and she told me to mind my own business. I've heard her and Aunty Ita gossiping about it, though. A couple of years ago, I watched the milkman deliver ten milk bottles to a neighbour in one go. He lined them up and asked me if I fancied a game of Skittles. I tried to laugh but could only manage a grunt. He hasn't spoken to me since.

There's a programme on the telly now called Tea Time with Tommy. Tommy sits at the piano for the show's duration and introduces various musical guests. He doesn't *play* the piano except at the end, though he occasionally fiddles with a music book as if he's *about* to play something. I don't think that he can read music. I probably shouldn't be critical, especially since

I'm not musical. Two weeks ago, O'Donnell surprised the class by producing three recorders, a tambourine, a triangle, and a pair of spoons that looked like they had been stolen from the school canteen. He gave me the triangle, and Crozier got the spoons. It was before the fart incident. The other boys quickly picked things up, but Crozier and I were useless. He told us to swap instruments at one stage, but that only worsened matters. Nothing happened every time I rattled my spoons. Crozier was supposed to strike his triangle *after* me but kept hitting it without waiting for the spoon sound. I understand he didn't want to wait all day, but he only made me look worse. I tried to make a joke out of the situation.

"*All I need now is a knife and fork*".

It didn't work.

"*The only fork you need is a bloody pitchfork, McCoubrey,*" barked O'Donnell. That was the end of my musical career.

Tommy has just introduced a group from Portstown called Dara and the Diamonds. My sister Lona shrieks desperately.

"Mammy, mammy, quick, it's Dara Batten and the Diamonds on TV. I can't believe it. She's in my class at school."

My mother rushes in, and the first thing she says is: "Woust, everybody woust." She and Lona are the only ones talkin', and I wish *they* would woust. Dara's group are singing a song called **Black Velvet Band**, and all four girls are wearing black nylon bands in their hair. They're smiling a lot, especially the one playing the triangle. Maybe she can teach me!

The first lines of the chorus are:

 Her eyes they shone like diamonds,
I thought her the queen of the land.

Dara isn't a bad wee singer; a big smile covers *her* face when she gets to the word *diamonds.* Her mouth looks like some of the keys on Tommy's piano. When the song's over, the McCoubrey household gives its verdict.

"At least they didn't let themselves down," says my mother.

"Their costumes were lovely."

"The costumes were gorgeous, weren't they," says Lona.

"She told me that they were going to wear something like that. I think she's a good singer, Mammy. She does have a good voice... now you can't say she hasn't."

Lona turns to Ben.

"She's in my class at school."

"Who?"

"Dara and the Diamonds."

"What, all of them?"

"No stupid, just Dara herself."

"He ate part of my friggin' Pars bun, or should I say, *Paris* Bun, you dimp."

Ben's gesturing at me.

"What's that got to do with Dara and the Diamonds, you wee skitter?"

Lona is getting agitated with Ben.

"Nothin'."

"Dara Batten's brother is in my class," I shout. "He pisses his pants every day."

Ben spits out a mouthful of Paris bun onto the carpet. He's roarin' with laughter.

"Maybe she can sing a song about that," he cries.

I'm in the toilet trying to lose weight. I never go in school, so I've been holding this one in all day. It's more satisfactory when there's a big one on its way. Don't get me wrong. I like pushing and grunting, especially when I have the Daily Mirror. Sometimes I start and then stop when I realise I've forgotten the newspaper. I hold the rest in until I return with the Mirror, or if I can't find it, anything with words on it. Provided that I can find something to read, I'm content. Even if it's a large one trying to force its way out, I keep it imprisoned for as long as possible, or at least until I've studied the racing page.

There's nothing readable in the house today, so I listen to the

Friday night noises outside the glazed bathroom window. Some mothers call their children in for tea, but the streets are quiet except for a few cars and a barking dog. I can hear our door again. It's not loud like the milkman's knock, and I wonder if anyone has heard it. Since we spend half our lives gazing through the window, I'm sure they've seen whoever it is that's knocking. Finally, I hear the door opening, and someone says, "Good evening, Mrs McCoubrey." It's the man from Hewitt and Gills.

He's early. I urgently pull the chain and wash my hands. I'm disappointed that I don't have time to examine my produce. Next time! When I reach downstairs, he's already sitting in the sitting room, studying his notebook to check how much we owe. He's about fifty, wears a tweed suit, and constantly pulls his trouser legs up at the knees. This way, they'll be good for a few more years. My mother is in the kitchen. She has left him alone for a few minutes and will return when ready. I sit down on the settee beside his chair. He acknowledges me.
"Hello".
I smile at him and say, "Hi." He pulls his trousers up and flicks through his notebook. If the pages get stuck, he licks his finger and turns them. I love it when the pages get stuck!
"Ah, there it is!"
He has found our bill and does a verbal count.
"Three and six, four and nine pence, five and six, seven shillings exactly."
My mother appears with her purse. "Here, take it out of that," she says, handing him a pound note.
"It comes to seven shillings, Mrs McCoubrey. Is that alright?" It's the same question that O'Donnell asked when he prevented me from playing football. What if she says: *"No, it's not alright?"*

She doesn't answer, and he counts the change with his gravelly voice.
"Thanks very much now. See you next week Mrs McCoubrey."
He puts the pound note into his bulging wallet. I'd love to know

how much is in there. It looks like hundreds.

"Bye-bye now."

The door opens, and he's gone. The sound of his voice lingers in my mind for a few seconds. It has tickled my sensations. I don't know why. Is it because he wears a cap and a tweed suit? Does his appearance demand that he's listened to? Is it simply the friendly tone, the *way* he says his words? I can't explain the buzz. But one thing is sure. I'm stimulated by the voice of a man who sells oilcloth.

McCoubrey is reading the news. It includes a report about farmers who sell fresh vegetables at the local markets. They're complaining about the price that the buyers are offering. Of course, farmers always complain, but I've never seen or heard of a poor one. Neither has my mother because I heard her saying it to one of the neighbours. At the end of the report, McCoubrey puts on his friendly face. "Ah, the poor old farmers," he sighs. "You know, looking at those vegetables reminds me of what the cabbage said to the caterpillar." He pauses. "I'll tell you what it said after the break."

Everyone in our house groans. No one tries to guess the answer. We're much too lazy for that. We know it's only a joke, but we don't have an intelligent contribution between us. If it was me telling the story, I'm sure that someone would manage to say *something.* Knowing our Ben, he'd tell me not to be stupid, as cabbages can't talk. Lona would listen intently, but she wouldn't know what a caterpillar was. There'd be no point in asking my ma because she's too busy to listen to jokes. I'd be too embarrassed to ask my da, in case he thought that the punch line wasn't funny. Honestly, I wouldn't tell anyone in our family a joke because I'm no good at it. That's why I leave it to the other McCoubrey.

The advertisements finish.

"Before the break, I asked you: *What did the cabbage say to the caterpillar?* I'm sure you're all patiently waiting for the answer."

We all shout in unison: "Will you come on, for God's sake." I say, *For frig's sake,* because I'm getting impatient.

"I wish he'd hurry up," says Lona, smiling at me. She's stuffing her face with Love Hearts, but she looks like she could manage half a Paris bun.

McCoubrey assumes a neutral expression.

"What did the cabbage say to the caterpillar?"

 Long pause.

 "You're always in my heart."

It's one of the corniest jokes I've ever heard.

"Oh, for God's sake, that's crap," I say. Ben is amused. Lona says that *she* has hearts. Love Hearts! I look at the TV, and Harry McCoubrey's face is beaming. He has cheered the whole country up for the weekend. When I return to school on Monday, I'll have cabbages and caterpillars coming out of my ears for a week. They'll have a field day, and no pun intended. Thanks, McCoubrey. Thanks for nothing.

Next is a programme called **Take Your Pick**. If the contestant answers specific questions correctly, they can choose a sum of money or decide to open one of the various boxes containing prizes. The prize could be a world cruise, five hundred pounds, a new car etc. If they choose the wrong box number, they get the "booby prize." It could be a pair of ladies' tights or a bunch of bananas. Tonight an old lady is answering the questions. She does well, and the compere Michael Miles teases her.

"What shall it be? £100, or do you want to take a chance and open the box? It's up to you now, but remember, you could get the booby prize."

The audience shouts, "Open the box." "Take the money." "Open the box." I swear that I can hear a man's voice shouting for both. My ma is watching.

"Take the money, Mrs," she urges. "That's what I'd do if I was you."

"Open the box," I scream. "Go on, open the box."

"If she opens the box, she might get the booby prize," cries Lona.

"That's what I'm hopin'."
"You're a bloomin' spoilsport," she says.

The old lady chooses number 13. The audience hushes. "Unlucky for some," cries Michael Miles, "but will number 13 be unlucky for you tonight? Let's go over and see."
He has this curious glint in his eye, and I wonder if she has chosen the booby prize. I hope so. The keys to the box are in his hand, and he's about to open it.
"Go on… let it be the booby prize…. please, the booby prize."
I'm shouting at the screen.
"Will you shut up," says my ma.
"I wish everybody'd shut up," chirps Lona.
Ben looks intense.
"And your prize is…..a weekend for two in Barbados."

Jammy git! I wanted her to win a pair of ladies' tights with ladders or a bunch of rotten bananas. Or a cash prize of £2! I only watch the programme to see people getting the booby prize. I *hate* it when people win. It doesn't matter how deserving they are. Nobody's more deserving than me. Sadly, she's got a friggin' holiday in Barbados, and I can't even get a cup of hot chocolate.

The lemonade man calls, and we get one white, one raspberry and two sarsaparillas. The first job is to hide two for my da. The other two are for us. The "us" still includes him. When he's suffering his hangover on Sunday mornings, the white cream soda bottle at the bedside provides respite. But, of course, if we have found it and taken a few sneaky slugs, there's uproar.
"Has anybody seen my friggin' lemonade?"
When this happens, I hide under the sheets and pretend I'm asleep. If the worst comes to the worst, I can blame it on Ben. I'm older than him.

"Barry-Joe, are you going to have a bath tonight?"
My ma is running the bath for the two younger ones.
"I had a bath last week."

"That was last week, and this is this week."

"And next week is next week."

"Don't you be cheeky, now."

"I'm not being cheeky. All I said is that next week is next week. So what's wrong with that?"

"You're starting to get on my nerves."

"How?"

"You're doin' it again."

"Doin' what?"

"I'll have your guts for garters."

"For God's sake. I'll take a bath tomorrow night."

"So you expect me to waste a whole bath full of water just because of you? Do you think we're made of money?"

"I can have half a bath."

"You only *half* wash yourself anyway. Don't you forget now... I'm warning ye, and make sure you wash behind your ears."

I can't work out if this means the back of my ears or the bit inside with all the wax.

Ben and Lona are already in the bath. Lona's packet of Love Hearts gets soaked, but she continues eating them. Ben is slapping the water vigorously. He thinks he's patting the dog. They keep losing the soap, which I find a few times for them. Finally, my mother arrives to wash their hair. She does it vigorously.

"There's soap in my eyes," cries Lona.

My ma rubs her eyes with a tea towel. She orders both out and dries Lona while Ben stands there shivering. I wonder why one can't stay in the bath until the other is dried. Wondering about it isn't enough, so I ask her.

"Why don't you dry them one at a time?"

"If I want your opinion, I'll ask for it."

"It's only common sense."

"Make yourself useful and go and make me a nice cup of tea."

"Alright, but it was just a suggestion."

She's glaring at me. All picture, no sound! When I say she likes to have the last word, it doesn't mean she has to open her mouth to achieve this. If looks could kill, I'd be stone-cold dead.

An eternity later, the children come downstairs wearing their pyjamas.
"The bath's ready, Barry-Joe. Hurry up, or the water will be cold."
My mother says this every week as if the bath water is actually still *warm.* I flee upstairs and run the hot tap until it turns tepid, then cold. I hop in and have my weekly wash. Momentarily I pretend I'm in the local swimming pool, but one stroke later, I bash my head against the bath taps. It's the shortest swim in history and the most painful.

I've almost forgotten to do the football pools for my da. The man from Littlewoods will be here in half an hour. I can't just pick out any old sixteen draws. It's crucial that I spend some time studying the teams and that I make deliberate choices. But, of course, it would be far quicker and better to choose the first sixteen numbers that enter my head. People who do this and don't know anything about football usually win. Those who study the form haven't a hope in hell. I stare intently at the coupon for half an hour. Each choice is agonising, but eventually, I pick sixteen matches. The aim is that at least eight of them will end in a draw. Then, checking that I have completed the coupon correctly about six times, I tick the "no publicity" box. My da doesn't want every Tom, Dick and Harry to hear about our good fortune. Nor me! None of us wants any begging letters from all the peasants in Portstown.

When I say I study the form, it's true, with one exception. I always mark *Oldham Athletic* down as a draw. It's because they're the only English team I have ever seen in the flesh. Last year they played a team called Glenavon from the next town. I took the bus to Lurgan by myself and watched the game. Oldham had an Irish player called Jimmy McIlroy, and Glenavon had a centre half called Wilbur Cush. I spent the entire game watching these two. They kicked lumps out of each other. At one stage, I overheard the guy next to me telling his mate that Wilbur Cush was his milkman. He was telling anyone who would listen and even some who wouldn't. I was tempted to ask him to give it out over the Tannoy system. I don't imagine *he* ticks the "no publicity" box on the football coupon. When Cush came near our side of the pitch, this guy would shout: "Don't forget to deliver our milk in the morning, Cush." He shouted it like it was a reminder. Maybe Cush played Skittles with his milk recently and won. The game ended in a 0 –0 draw, but what struck me most, apart from the milkman, was that Oldham wore orange skips. Oldham Orangemen! I couldn't believe it.

I sometimes wonder if the man from Littlewoods keeps the Pools' money for himself. He's one of those sincere-looking guys who looks *too* honest. I prefer it when he comes in the wintertime because then he wears a flat cap pulled down over his forehead. It makes him look a bit dodgy, but I trust him more like this. He gets tonight's money, even without his cap. I rush into the kitchen to make another cup of tea for my ma. She forgot to drink the previous one because she had a lie down after bathing the children. It was supposed to be for ten minutes but lasted half an hour. My da has just arrived home from work via the pub. I'm relieved he looks pretty sober, and I add another cup. As usual, he marches into the kitchen and isn't too pleased to see the dog lying on the settee.

"Get to hell down o' that," he says, sitting down where Sonny was lying.

"Somebody lock that bloody dog in the coal shed".

He settles down to read the local paper, the Portstown Times.
My mother hears him from the sitting room. She's sitting on the window seat, looking out the window.

"Whose turn is it to lock the dog in the coal shed?"

   She looks at me.

"I did it last night."

"And I did it the night before and the night before that."

Lona can always go one better than everyone else. She takes after her ma.

"Alright, I'll do it after I've drank my tea," I say. "Mind you, Lona, you're not even drinking tea like the rest of us. So nothing is stoppin' *you* from locking the dog in the coal shed."

"That's because you never made me any tea. I didn't want any, but that's not the point. You could've asked."

"What's the point of askin' if you're only goin' to say no? Anyway, you're drinkin' lemonade."

"That doesn't mean I couldn't drink tea at the same time if I wanted to."

"I thought you've just said you didn't want any."

My mother butts in. "If you two don't stop arguin', I'll friggin' lock the both of *you* in the coal shed, along with the dog."

Indian Reservation Army

"Rosemary, have you read about that eejit Riney?"
It's my da coming into the sitting room, newspaper in hand. He's addressing my ma, but I'm listening, and I prise the paper from him. Not too hard, just a steady tug until he lets go. The article he's referring to is about a local twenty-year-old called Aidan Riney. We know him as Fiddler Riney. He has just been sentenced to six months gaol for writing the words **IRA** on a factory roof. He claimed in court that the letters stood for "*Indian Reservation Army*". The judge didn't believe him. Riney claimed he had a longstanding interest in the Indian tribes and supported their cause. Unfortunately for him, Riney comes from the Tunnel area of Portstown. It's well known for its Republican sympathisers. Judging by the graffiti in the Tunnel, there must be hundreds of Indian Reservation Army supporters living there, as well as Riney.

My father tells my ma about Riney.
"That's a good'un, Indian Reservation Army. I wonder how long it took him to think that one up."
"Is that the same Riney that dances with the stools down at the Yacht?"
"That's him, alright. His head's cut. He's a real head the ball."
"He mustn't be right in the head. Sure, the judges aren't stupid. They know fine rightly what he meant. It's a pity he couldn't have told them something better than that."
"Like what?"
"I don't know. Anything but that?"
"It's the dearest tin of paint he'll ever buy, I'll tell you that."
"He won't be buying any more for a while, so he won't."

Two months gaol for each letter! Whatever he was writing, he should at least have written it in full. If he *is* a "head the ball", maybe he *does* have some quaint interest in the Indian reservations. I'm trying to convince myself. It's just that I don't think that judges are mind readers. How the hell do they know what other people think? They're only interested in what *they* believe. If someone wrote **UVF** and claimed it stood for the Ulster Veterinary Force instead of the Ulster Volunteer Force, would they still get six months? What would the judges think then? I'm starting to understand the meaning of discrimination and double standards. I hope that Fiddler *stole* the paint that did the damage. In for a penny, in for a pound! I remind myself to mention these evil thoughts at confession tomorrow.

I give Sonny water from the empty Fray Bentos tin that was my father's dinner. He slurps at it for at least a minute. Then I lock him in the coal shed. I hear him scratching at the coal shed door when I go upstairs to the bedroom. I look outside and see a man's black shoe on the shed roof. It looks old and dusty, but I can't see any holes. There's no sign of its companion. Every month I notice odd footwear. Once, I counted four shoes, three slippers and two water boots. None of them matched. They never do.

I try to read a bit of my book - *Around the World in Eighty Days*. My ma and da got it last Christmas, but I haven't progressed much. I could've been around the world twice by now. After a few pages, I give up. Friday is a do-nothing day, and that includes reading. I'll continue my journey later.

Ben is sprawled across both sides of the bed. I slip in against the wall. I'll have to clamber over him if I need to go for a piss during the night. Some boys at school call it pish, but I think this is a crude word. I never use it. Mackie always uses it when trying to beat his record: "Stand back, boys. Mackie's about to have a pish." He loves introducing his act. If they use this word, it tells you something about a person's personality. Not good! As I drift off to sleep, I hear Sonny having another little scratch at the coal shed door.

The coal man wakes me up at seven o'clock in the morning. I hear the thunder as the black stuff is emptied into our coal shed, hoping that Sonny has escaped before being buried alive. His barking provides reassurance. I feel under my legs. Thankfully it's dry. Then I feel Ben's pyjamas. They are also dry, but he's annoyed. "Leave me alone, you fruit, will ye," he shrieks. He turns away and continues snoring. Once I'm awake, that's it. I head downstairs, where my da is making breakfast. Examining the contents of the frying pan, I notice two sausages, a piece of bacon, a bit of soda bread and a slice of potato bread. Is nobody else having breakfast except me? Am I the only one who's hungry this morning? Are ye not having anything yourself? I think about asking one of these questions but decide not to.

"Who the heck are the Oldham Orangemen?"
He's smirkin' at me.
"What are you talkin' about?"
"You told me and your ma all about the Orangemen from Oldham last night."
"When?"
"About three o'clock in the morning."
"I was sleeping then."
"You were sleeping alright, bloody sleepwalkin'."
"I don't believe ye."
"You're lucky you didn't fall down the stairs. You said that you wanted the Oldham Orangemen to draw. That's the last time I'm lettin' you fill in the friggin' football coupon. I'll do it myself from now on."
"I can't remember a thing."
"We made you go to the toilet. Can you remember that?"
"Sort of."
"Sort of, my ass. You were pissin' all over the place, so I had to hold your buddly to keep it straight."
"Shut up, will ye."
"I had to hold it for ye. Otherwise, you'd have stunk the place

out."

"I hope you washed your hands then. Is there any breakfast for me?"

I'm embarrassed. It's usually against my nature to be easily embarrassed, but the shame of gibbering about Oldham in my sleep is with me. It's bad enough to sleepwalk, but *sleep-talking* is another matter. I could at least have chosen *Celtic* to talk about, but as they're my team, I want them to *win*, not draw. Or Manchester United. I don't support them, but they have this exciting Irish player, George Best, in their team. So I don't want it to be a draw whenever he's playing. Mind you, when he does play, there seldom *is* a draw.

He touched my buddly! Jesus, I'll never live that one down. His dirty hands on my buddly! I'm the only one in my class that calls it a "buddly." Tiddler, dangler, chopper, welt, wire, slasher, cock. They've all been used to describe it. The Milky Bar Kid, who reads the Dandy, calls it a penis. When I was younger and was about to wet myself, I would rush into the toilet, and if my father was in there having a piss, I'd have no choice but to share the bowl. I used to have a sneaky look at his buddly and then cover mine up.

I've developed this habit of not swallowing fried food unless I'm sipping tea simultaneously. My ma and da make milky tea for the children and proper tea for themselves. We only get half a cup. Theirs is full to the brim. I hate being treated the same as our Lona. I only get a full cup when I make it myself, go to my granny McCoubrey's house, or visit my cousin Turtler's. He's the tea maestro. He lets it stew for five minutes and pours it about two feet above the mug. Turtler doesn't believe in cups. His cha, as he calls it, is bubbly, hot and strong. It tastes like tea. I like things that taste like they ought to. So does Turtler.

I reread the article about Fiddler Riney. If I like a piece, I read it several times. The words don't change, but my enjoyment does. I wonder if anyone from the Council has painted over the offensive graffiti. Maybe they leave it there for the next person sentenced to six months in gaol. I've heard about killing two birds with one stone. Perhaps they imprison two people with the same tin of paint. I'll see if Fiddler's artwork is still there later on.

I've got a few little jobs before I get my pocket money. Firstly I have to tidy the coal shed. Our house is obsessed with the damn coal shed. The slack the coal man leaves always spills over the wooden barrier that's supposed to prevent this from happening. It's not that we order too much slack. The coal men deliver coal the same way I go for a piss when I'm in a hurry. People can either like it or lump it. Sonny's a mousy-coloured dog, and one Saturday, he emerged looking as black as the ace of spades. We changed his name to Sooty for that day, but he refused to respond to it unless there was food involved. After our weekly bath, we washed and shampooed him in the same water. The water didn't change colour *that* much.

My second job is to tidy the bedroom. Sometimes I feel like doing without my pay rather than enduring this purgatory. It's so hateful that words fail me. What's even more odious than tidying the room is *thinking about tidyin'* the damn room. It's painful, and I could avoid some of this pain if I got a move on, but I'm addicted to thinking. Sometimes I make a good start and feel compelled to sit down and agonise about what's left. Cleaning the bedroom can take two hours on a bad day; even then, I sometimes make a right hames of it.

I Confess

My chores are over, though it's a little congested under my bed. I'm in the sitting room watching my da, who's making me wait for my pay. He glances at me a few times, but I continue reading the article about Fiddler. He puts on his donkey jacket. My head stays buried in the paper. He takes his coat off again. I hate it when people act like they don't know whether they're coming or going. He's going nowhere, and we both know it. I put my coat on and sit down again. I'm off to confession like a good Catholic boy.

"Where are ye goin'?"

"To confession."

"At this time?"

"It's almost ten o'clock."

"Did I give you anything last night?"

I feel like saying: *nothing apart from a tug on the buddly.*

"I don't think so."

He rattles the change in his pocket and pulls out half a crown and two shilling coins. He gives me one shilling, pauses to witness the look of misery on my face, and then gives me the other. The half-crown coin is for decoration purposes only. He casually returns it to the safety of his pocket.

"Thanks."

He stares at me. I friggin' hate this part, having to say thanks. I know I should be grateful, but I'm not. To me, "thanks" is the same as rolling around the floor, begging him to take pity on a poor penniless soul. It's like saying: *Listen, I know that you're the man of the house who gets up every morning at a quarter to six while I'm still dreaming about Oldham Orangemen, who works all week come rain or snow, while I pick my nose and do frig all about the house, but it would be appreciated if you could spare me a tiny bit of your hard-earned cash.*

Let's be honest here. It's like saying: *Anything for the Black Babies* and hoping that he doesn't respond like Crozier did one day in school - with a bar of Lifebuoy soap.

It's funny how money changes people's moods. The click of the two silver shilling coins in my trousers cheers me. I keep my hand in my pocket for safety reasons. I'm not the sort who loses money as I'm ultra-careful. Indeed I'm paranoid about losing things. I lost a pencil once in school and spent the whole day searching for it. During my search, I found another that was better, an HB one. Small consolation! Firstly, it wasn't mine; secondly, somebody else must have found *mine* and kept it. I hate the thought of other people having what's mine, even when I have something that might be *theirs.* It's just the way I am.

It's almost confession time. I mustn't forget about hoping that Fiddler stole the paint. These are sinful thoughts, if not an actual sin itself. The other sins are the usual venial ones. It wasn't my fart that scared the waxwings, so I won't have to face the discomfort of telling that. Good luck, Crozier! Mind you, he's a genuine rebel, so he probably won't bother to admit it unless he gets Father Quinlan. Crozier's the type of fella that wouldn't be averse to releasing one when he's in the confession box. I'm not saying he would go as far as to blame it on the priest, but he's capable of doing these things with a straight face. If he could control the expression on his bum cheeks as much as the one on his face, he would encounter less trouble in life.

I join a long queue on the chapel's hard wooden benches beside the confession boxes. The latter are at the chapel's side; each box has three separate doors. The middle door belongs to the priest, and the confessors take their places on either side. While waiting my turn, I try to work out the logic of two separate queues. Most of those going in on the right are women. My side has men - young and old. I notice old Lazareth at the front of the row. *Christ, he's not taking any chances, is he*? I can't imagine what *he* has to confess. Maybe he was late for Mass one day last week. I certainly don't believe that he harbours any evil thoughts. I stare at him. He seems slightly worried about something, though I don't know what it could be. I catch his gaze. There's something beautiful about his red, watery eyes. He's lived his life, and it is two minutes to midnight. I think that old Lazareth is impatient for the clock to tick faster. Most people are paranoid about dying. He's paranoid about *living.*

It's my turn. I enter the box. It is pitch black. It feels like a stationary ghost train. I can hear muffled sounds from the other side. The priest's voice is much louder than the confessor's, but I can't make out his words. I'm trying to, and also straining to listen to the confessor. She must be a sinner because she's been there for five minutes. I hear a bit of commotion. Things get noisy, and before I can compose myself, the iron grill in front of my face slams open, and I am facing a big bald head. My trial has begun.

"Bless me, Father, for I have sinned. It's been a month since my last confession." I take a deep breath.

"Tell me your sins."

He has put me on the spot. I feel like a sinner before I've confessed anything.

"I've been telling lies...I stole some biscuits from home.....I was arguing with my ma.....I was fighting in school.....I looked at a dirty magazine ...I stole some biscuits from our house...."

He interrupts me.

"That's the second time you've confessed to stealing biscuits, son. Once is enough for each sin."

"I know, Father, but the thing is, the first ones were assorted, and the second were plain."

"Are you trying to be derogatory in the house of God?"

"No, Father, I'm only telling the truth. The first ones were those plain Marie ones, and the second ones were from one of those boxes we only usually get at Christmas. All different types."

"This is not the place to be insolent. Now about the magazine. Did you look at it, or did you study it?"

"I looked at it for about ten seconds.........twice."

"You seem to like doing things twice.....for your penance I want you to say a decade of the Rosary.....twice...and to do the Stations of the Cross. Go in peace."

He makes a cross sign with the edge of his left palm and slams the shutter closed. I'm back in my black ghost train, with only my penance for baggage.

I stumble out of the black box, gasping for air. Two decades of the Rosary and the Stations of the Cross! I haven't stabbed anyone, robbed or raped anyone. I've stolen a few biscuits from my house when nobody was lookin'. I've had a scrap and had a peep at someone's diddies. Christ, it's an awful price—no time to waste. I kneel and rush through the first decade of the Rosary. I had been expecting an *Our Father and Three Hail Marys*, but this is purgatory. I mutter the second decade at one hundred miles an hour. Time to find the Stations of the Cross! I know fourteen exist, but finding the correct order is a nightmare. It's like walking down one of those hateful streets where the numbers don't make sense. Finally, I locate them and pray from 1 to 7. I then decide I've had enough, so I leave.

However, as I walk away from the chapel, guilt grabs me by the short and curlies, dragging me back in anguish to finish what I've started. I have that "tidying the bedroom" sensation again. Only when I have brushed the guilt from the slate will I be able to relax. I find 8,9,10,11, and 12. 13 and 14 are in a remote corner of the chapel, and it takes me ten excruciating minutes to find them. It's like thinking you've finished the bedroom cleaning, and then your mother comes in and says: *What about under the bed?* You don't tell her that's where you've been putting half the dirt. There's no escape from women, priests and God. In that order!

I *do* feel cleaner after my penance. A Saturday surge ripples through me, and it feels good to be alive. I dander towards the town centre. On the other side of Chapel Street, I notice Tam

McShane, the headmaster of our school. He's leaving the tailor's shop. Teachers don't usually use the main streets in Portstown. They sneak around the side streets or pop into the chapel. Maybe McShane has been saying the Stations of the Cross too. I hope his geography is better than mine. He's a teacher, so it should be. Passing the indoor market, I see people scrambling for bargains. They only do this because it's called the *Market*. Most of the stuff there is rubbish, apart from the fruit from the stall that sells apples, oranges and bananas. Although I'm casually dandering, my legs are on automatic pilot towards Woolworths. It's at the bottom of the town, so I have the glamour of a stroll down Portstown Way. Shoe shops, a paper shop, a linen shop, a high street bank, Liptons the grocers, a few pubs, a home bakery, a couple of clothes shops specialising in school uniforms, and a TV repair shop. A blissful town centre!

Lots of strangers say hello to prove how friendly they are. Catholics and Protestants greet each other as if there's no difference. If you've seen one shopping bag, you've seen them all. A friendly voice greets me. "Hi ya, Barry-Joe." It's my Aunty Aileen. This is going to be an exciting conversation.
"Hi ya, Aileen."
"Where's your mammy?" she asks.
I feel like saying: "Let me think about that for a wee minute," for she's bound to be in the house or out shopping. One of the two! Otherwise, she's gone missing.
"I think she's in the house."
"Are you just up the town for a walk?"
"Yeah, I'm just having a quick stroll."
"It's nice weather for this time of the year, isn't it?"
I want to remind her that it's supposed to be the beginning of summer. I don't.
"Aye, it's not too bad at all."
"Well, sure, I'll see you later."
"Ok."
I move on.

"Barry-Joe, come 'ere a minute."
I move back.
"Me and Paddy are going to see Big Tom and the Mainliners at St. Mary's Hall next Saturday. Would you be interested in mindin' the children? I'm having terrible trouble gettin' anyone proper to do it."
I'm not sure whether I count as proper or not.
"Will, if you don't mind, then I don't mind. I'll do it, surely."
  I smell money.
"Sure, I'll talk to ye before then. Cheerio now Barry-Joe."

I head straight to Woolworths with a spring in my step and two shilling coins in my pocket. Once inside, I walk twice around the perimeter (the priest was right), eyeing up the biscuit counter. I glimpse what I came here for. However, the problem is that I know one of the girls on the till. She's the sister of a guy in my class, and she's posh. Not too posh to work in Woolworths, but posh. I look down at my jeans. They haven't been washed for three months. I try to remember whether I've washed my face this morning. I finger it, but that doesn't answer my question. Yes, I think I did. I don't stop pawing it, anxiously hoping no one will notice my dirty trousers.

Circling the biscuit counter, I watch the queue like a hawk. It's all about timing. I'm trying to judge it so that the other girl, the ugly one, serves me. Having counted the number of people in the queue, I join the back of it. I'm hiding behind women with varicose veins and net shopping bags. It looks like I've judged it right. Posh Girl is about to finish serving an old lady, and the person in front of me is next. The old biddy receives her change and stares at it for about a minute. Finally, Posh Girl intervenes and tries to reassure her by counting it all out again, coin by coin.
The ugly one is still busy.
Hurry up, come on, will ye, for God's sake.

The old lady is reassured. She thanks Posh Girl and starts talking about the weather because she appreciates her helpfulness.

"Nice day for this time of the year, isn't it?"

I'm getting desperate because *Ugly Girl* has almost finished with *her* customer, who doesn't seem interested in the weather.

"For cryin' out loud, will ye hurry up"?

I can't contain these words. The woman in front of me looks round and shrugs her shoulders. She's one of those patient types who always irritate me. Posh continues to take her time with the old dear. Soon, the *Not Posh* worker finishes serving, and the calm person ahead of me approaches the biscuit counter. Now I'm at the front of the queue. Finally! Two seconds later, Posh is saying cheerio to her customer, and I have no choice but to step forward. I've lost. The good-looking sister of my classmate confronts me. She recognises me and is quite friendly.

"What would you like"?

I know *exactly* what I would like if I was a bit older. She looks like Julie Christie in *Far from the Madding Crowd*. Her only "blemish" is a mole on her left cheek, which makes her more attractive. I'm only twelve, so she can afford to look at me as if I'm just a boy, and she does. Do I act like an adult and buy a pound of *whole* custard creams, or do I order what I came here for? I stare at the inviting boxes of whole fresh biscuits: custard creams, fig rolls, chocolate digestives, bourbon creams, chocolate wafers and jam tarts.

I deliberate. She smiles faintly.

"As a matter of interest, do you have any *broken* biscuits?"

It's a ridiculous question since they are piled high in the tin tray in front of me.

"Yes."

Her smile feels like laughter.

"Can I just have three-pence worth, please?"

She scoops a cluster of broken biscuits from the tray and gradually drops them into a paper bag. Then, when the weighing scale dial indicates precisely one pound, she glances at me and throws an extra broken biscuit into the bag. I'm glad of the extra one, but she might as well have laughed in my face. She might as well have left her counter, marched over to the store Tannoy, and made an important announcement: "Barry-Joe McCoubrey has just bought three-pence worth the broken biscuits... wee Barry-Joe McCoubrey and his wee bag of broken biscuits." I pay her with one of my shilling coins and get a sixpence and a three-penny bit in change. Then, head lowered, I slither towards the exit, clutching my white bag and my pride.

Once outside, I can unwind again. Buying broken biscuits can be a stressful business. I peep into the white paper bag to see how many broken biscuits are *whole.* There're a few whole ones in there. I can see lots of chocolate and caramel pieces and only a few of those plain ones that, for some strange reason, are called Nice biscuits. What's *nice* about them? I secure the bag and lengthen my stride. Then I weave past people gossiping about mundane things. Some of the gossipy men are worse than the bloomin' women. They also tend to be plump (from food, not booze), jolly-looking rather than good-looking, and clothed in something checked. It could be the trousers, the jacket, or maybe even their underpants, but it's checked. None of these men is of building site calibre. Nor factory material! They probably work in a nursery, a dry cleaning shop, or are claiming the bru. They look like respectable working-class people, but some have probably stolen things. I see that self-righteous cunning streak running across their eyes. I see it when they gossip and when they wear their checked coats. There are no flies on these guys.

Someone jumps on my back and stays there.
"Go on Arkle, go on Arkle, go on Arkle."
My bag of biscuits drops to the ground. I twist around aggressively. It's Crozier.
"Frig you Crozier, what are you friggin' playin' at. Look what you've done now, for Christ's sake. You've friggin' broken my broken biscuits, so you have."
I pick the bag up.

"If these are broken, it's all over the friggin' head of you."

"Don't be stupid, McCoubrey. How can you break broken biscuits?"

"Some of them are whole ones."

"I don't give a fiddler's fuck whether they're whole, broken, or in little bits. If it's a bag of crumbs you've got there, I'll still eat them. So hurry up, will ye. I'm starvin'."

Crozier ordered some broken biscuits a few weeks ago, and the girl told him they only had whole ones. "In that case, can you break me a few," he said. And she did!

The broken biscuits aren't broken too much. One of the whole ones has split in two, but the other few have survived. This is crucial because a bag of broken biscuits, without any whole ones, is like jelly without ice cream. So I give Crozier a handful of broken ones and take a whole one, plus some broken ones, for myself. The thought of giving him a whole one doesn't exist.

I'm surprised to see Crozier up the town. He usually sticks to his area.

"What are ye doing up here anyway?"

"I can't talk with my mouth full."

"You make up for it when your mouth's not full, so you do."

"You can talk."

"That's because my mouth's not full like yours. Are you headin' home now?"

"Aye."

"I'll go with you because I want to see the graffiti on the roof."

"You mean Fiddler's?"

"Aye! Is it still there?"

"Yeah, but it's been crossed out. You can still make the letters out, though. Give me a few more of those, will ye."

"I'll give you a few nice ones."

I give him a handful of *Nice* ones.

"What's nice about these flippin' things? Where's the friggin' chocolate ones?"

"The ones I gave you *are* Nice."

"Ha, friggin' ha. Come on. A few chocolate ones."

"If I had a few coffee ones, I'd give you them."

"Are you still goin' on about that hot chocolate?"

"You and McGann are friggers for doing that... I was sickened."

"I know you were. We were pissin' ourselves."

I relent and give him a few chocolate ones and another *Nice* one. Then, I give myself the same. I don't want to leave all the plain ones to the last.

"Here, McCoubrey, I've got a good one for ye."

"Go on then."

"There's this girl in a field in America, down on her hunkers having a crap. This fella walks past and shouts over: *Are you shitin' honey?* So the girl shouts back: *Get outta here...do you think I'm a flippin' bumblebee?*"

I laugh heartily. Partly because it's funny and partly because Crozier's roarin' at his joke. A wry smile or a grunted guffaw won't suffice.

"That's a good'un, alright."

We turn into Woodhouse Street, past a jolly-looking man in a checked blazer. He's chattering to a woman who's twice his age.

"Look at yer man, Crozier. He's like a real auld doll."

 "I know. He should shut his mouth and give his ass a chance."

The Tunnel

We head towards the Tunnel area. Crozier lives here. We enter under a dark narrow railway bridge. It feels like I'm in one of those tunnels you go through on the train, except I'm not on a train. It doesn't occur to me that the area's known as the *Tunnel* precisely for this reason. Other people from the past have felt the same sensation as me and christened the place the Tunnel. Officially there's no such place. If you sent a letter to someone in the Tunnel, it would return marked "address unknown". Crozier lives in an area that doesn't exist!

When you enter a place like the Tunnel, you anticipate some action. Something about passing through this particular tunnel inspires expectation and excitement. I'm a deep thinker for my age, but I haven't thoroughly analysed it yet. The Tunnel is the only Catholic area in Portstown, so I can walk freely here without being accosted because of my religion. There's no danger of my broken biscuits being kicked out of my hands. Children might beg me for some of them, but that's ok. If I get fed up with it, I can stick them up my jumper (biscuits). The common denominator down here is poverty. As long as you don't look too prosperous or too Protestant, you can pass through in one piece.

Crozier is safe because he lives in this tube of terraced houses. We pass a grocer's shop at the neck of the tunnel. More people are milling about outside than inside. Most of them are young boys eating gobstoppers. I see a man in a brown coat cutting cheese with a piece of string. There's a new supermarket called Liptons in the town centre, which sells cheese in plastic packets. They don't have a string man.
"I've got a wee surprise for you," says Crozier.
"I hope it's not the same one you gave the waxwings."

"Just follow me," he says. I follow him as far as the bookie's shop. He pulls out a tiny piece of crinkled paper from his back pocket. A betting docket!

"Did you win anything?"

"Just watch this."

He sticks his head around the open door of the betting shop and calls someone by wagging his finger at him. A man in a green checked suit and a cravat appears.

"Collect this for me, will you, Eddie?"

Eddie unravels the docket and looks at it for about three minutes.

"Three winners out of four, and the other one should have won … it would have hacked up if it had a jockey riding it."

I look at Crozier.

"Did your horse not have a jockey?"

"Of course it had a jockey, but he was friggin' useless. That's what he meant."

Eddie goes back inside. He returns five long minutes later, clasping something in his left fist. Crozier cups his hands, and I watch three two-bob coins, a one-bob coin, and a sixpence drop. "There was seven and six off it," says Eddie. Then he looks Crozier in the eyes and pushes the open palm of his right hand forward. Crozier lets it dangle there for a few minutes. Then he sets a tanner into it. Eddie doesn't budge. His face reddens, but he doesn't speak. Crozier smirks at me, retrieves his tanner and replaces it with the shilling coin. Eddie still doesn't budge until Crozier says: "That's your last, Mrs Lafferty." Eddie withdraws his hand and escapes to the betting shop with his tip.

I feel like putting *my* hand out. Crozier checks his winnings. I don't like the way he's looking at that tanner. No worries. He flicks a two-bob bit into the air for me to catch. It doesn't hit the ground. I offer him the remaining whole broken biscuits, and he accepts.

"Where's Fiddler's graffiti?"

"It's round the corner, on top of Denny's."

We drift round the corner, and sure enough, there it is. I'm surprised that the letters are still easily read. They are as clear as day, except for a horizontal line across the middle. It's the type of mark O'Donnell would make if he wanted to indicate a mistake. I turn to Crozier.

"Imagine getting six months for that."

"Getting six *weeks* for that! He's not all there, that Fiddler fella."

"What do you think about this Indian Reservation Army crack?"

"When he gets out, I hope he goes and joins them and doesn't come back. He's a grade A head-the-ball, that boy."

"He must be all right."

"Did you know that Fiddler has the biggest welt in Portstown?"

"You're jokin'."

"He has this trick where he makes a hole in his trouser pocket and asks girls to search for something by pretending that his arm is broken and that he can't reach in. When they do, they end up feeling his chopper. I've heard it's almost as big as a Swiss Roll."

"You're havin' me on… as big as a Swiss Roll? Jesus! Do you mean lengthways or across?"

"Both."

Paris buns and Swiss rolls! My head is spinning.

"Is that your granda, McCoubrey?"

Across the road, I see an old guy in a navy pin-striped suit walking crookedly. "He's as pissed as a fart," slags Crozier. "You'd know all about that," I reply. Crozier's right; Granda McCoubrey *is* very drunk. He stops at a lamppost to talk to himself. It seems to be an interesting conversation. His trousers are hanging down. He must have forgotten his belt because he's a brilliant tailor who's very fussy about his two suits. He starts to fiddle with his flies. "The old blurt's going to take a piss," laughs Crozier. I'm laughing too, but I hope he keeps his pecker in its place. My granda moves up the Tunnel in search of another pub. I decide to visit Granny McCoubrey, now that he's out of the house.

However, it's a bit ignorant to leave Crozier after he's just given me two bob.

"I might go and visit my granny McCoubrey," I say meekly. "Do you want to come?"

The last thing I want is Crozier or anybody else to come with me. Visiting relatives is a personal thing. I want to relax and have my usual Granny McCoubrey experience. Grannies aren't for sharing with anybody else unless you're family. "Nah," he says. "I'm going to hang round the bettin' shop for a while. I'll see you on Monday, sure. I don't think we'll be seeing those waxwings, though." He smirks, and we part, Crozier towards the bookies and me across the road to Granny McCoubrey's.

Granny McCoubrey is at home. She always is. Thankfully she's alone. I hate it when other people interrupt my visits. They walk in casually as if nothing's happening, but *everything's* happening. My happiness is being disturbed. Before I sit down, she offers me a cup of tea, and I notice an open packet of McVities digestive biscuits on the table. Who can turn down a full cup of tea with whole biscuits? She disappears into the scullery, and soon, an enticing smell of gas and brewing tea wafts into the living room.

"How are you doin', son... it's good to see ye. Have you been up the town?"

I tell her I have but don't mention the broken biscuits. They're mostly in my (and Crozier's) belly, but some small bits are still in the white paper bag hidden inside my jacket. She's wearing an apron, and a brave smile is etched on her worn face. Her silver hair and saucer eyes make her look attractive. I bet you she was good-looking when she was young. She settles me down with a full mug of brown tea and an open packet of digestive biscuits. I wish I'd kept my broken biscuits for later, as I can't maximise the enjoyment from these digestives. I'll just have to do the best I can. Sparks are coming off the fire's peat briquettes, *Grandstand* is on the telly, and I'm about to dip my first digestive. I feel happy.

"Did you see your granda on your travels?"

Do I tell her that he was propping up a lamppost outside and seemed stotious, or do I tell a little lie? It's too soon, after my confession, to start telling lies. So I decide to keep the slate clean for a bit longer.

"I think I saw him walking up the Tunnel. I'm not one hundred per cent sure, but I think that it might have been him."

"I suppose he was drunk, was he?"

She is wearing a sad smile.

"I'm not sure...it's hard to tell."

I won't tell her he was as drunk as a fart and didn't know what day it was. She knows what he's like, so there's no point in confirming what she already knows.

"How's your mother and father?"

"They're fine. I think they're going out tonight."

"Your mother's a good woman, ye know, and your father's a great worker."

"I know."

I've heard these lines before, but she always says it as if she means it. I agree with her views on my ma and da, but it's not something I like to dwell on. It's easier to take her word for it.

"Is that somebody knocking at your door?"

"It could be anybody," she says, lifting herself off the couch. I listen intently, feeling calm and relaxed. The voices at the doorstep seem to echo through the hall. My granny is talking to a well-spoken man. He can't be from around here. I've heard that voice before. She's bringing him into the house. I stop slouching in my chair and conceal the packet of digestives underneath the cushion. A man in a dog collar and black suit comes in. I don't believe my eyes. It's Father McGrane, the priest who took my confession an hour and a half ago. I pray to God that he doesn't recognise me. I had a good view of *him* because there was a dim light in his part of the confession box, but I was in pitch darkness, and he hardly looked at me. Surely to God, he won't recognise me.

"This is my grandson Father."

My granny looks proud. She offers the priest a cup of tea.

"I'm only after one," he replies.

"One's all you're gettin'," I mutter.

She brings him one anyway, in a cup and saucer. I've sneaked the digestives into the scullery so she can put them on a plate for the priest. He soaks his biscuit into the tea without a hint of embarrassment and washes it down with a long slurp that empties half the cup. He must think that he's at Mass, drinking wine. He smiles gently at me and asks me what school I go to. He knows O'Donnell well. "A fine teacher," he says, "a fine teacher indeed." I nod in agreement. O'Donnell *is* a good teacher, but he puts the fear of God into ye. Maybe that's what the priest calls "fine". Finally, he mentions "trousers and turn-ups". My granny leaves the living room. I hear her hoking vigorously.

Soon she returns.

"I'm very sorry, Father, there's no sign of them. Everything's a mess in there, but I'm sure they're somewhere. Hughy shouldn't be too long; he's probably put them somewhere safe."

"How long do you think he'll be Mrs McCoubrey? It's just that I need the trousers for ten o'clock mass tomorrow morning?"

"I'll tell you what, Father." She turns to me. "Barry-Joe, son, would you go and see if you can find your granda? He can't have gone far."

She shows me to the door. "Have a look in Hagan's pub," she whispers, "and tell him that the priest's here waitin' on his trousers."

I scamper out quickly. A few minutes later, I'm outside the pub. I ask a man going in to get Hughy McCoubrey for me.

You mean *Cughy* McCoubrey?"

"Yeah."

I hate it when Portstown people mispronounce words. It's as if they're happy to stay in the gutter. My Granny McCoubrey told me half an hour ago that she'd just finished cleaning the *windies* and washing the *flure.* She calls Portstown "*Portiestown*". Most of the people around here have the same attitude to pronunciation. They like to *mispronounce.* Especially here in the Tunnel! Why say Hughy when you can get away with Cughy? Well, frig the whole lot of them. I'm looking for Hughie McCoubrey and nobody else but Hughie.

Out he comes. He doesn't look surprised, just drunk.
"Hello, son, did you want me? Which one are you?"
"Barry-Joe."
"Barry-Joe, who?"
"Barry-Joe McCoubrey."
"Pardon me, son. You're Danny's eldest fella. Aye, that's right. Here come on in, and I'll buy ye a drink…. I'll buy you a bottle of stout, so I will."
"Listen for a second. The priest is in your house looking for his trousers. He left them in to get them turned up, and he's there now lookin' for them."
"C'mon in for a wee bottle of stout…I won't tell yer da I even saw ye."
"I'm too young to get in, and anyway, what about the priest's turn-ups?"
He eyeballs me with a glazed, slightly disdainful stare.
"What about them? I've got a turn-up for him, alright. I've got a right turn-up for the priest."
"What do ye mean?"
"I mean that his bloody turn-ups are in the pawn shop up the town, and if he needs them for tomorrow, he's goin' to have to pay a pound note for the privilege. Which day is tomorrow anyway?"
I look at him in amazement. *Jesus Christ, he's pawned the priest's trousers.*

Back at Granny's house, I give her the news at her front door. "Jesus Mary and Saint Joseph," she declares. Her saucer eyes are looking through me, and I wish I could say something to ease the pain. I can't. I wait outside while she gives the priest the bad news. She's crying as she shows him out. Father McGrane's bald head is beetroot red, and his face spells *GRIM.* Darry could spell it correctly if he were here. I watch until he disappears from view. I'm delighted. *Two Decades of the Rosary and the Stations of the Cross for me. The pawn shop for you. Slap it up ye.*

I try to console Granny by making her a cup of tea. Then there's a knock.

"Can you get that dure, son?"

It's her daughter Lizzie. Time for me to fade out! If I'm going to console people, I like to do it alone. So why does another person arrive to steal the glory when you're trying to be helpful?

On my way home, I pass a stocky teenager standing outside a sweetshop, tapping anyone entering or leaving. "Have you any odds?" I hear him ask a woman who's as old as my granny.

"Yeah, I've got two odd socks on me. Is that any good to ye?"

He laughs and, spying me, asks the same question. I'm tempted to offer him the rest of the broken biscuits, but he's a big boy. I check my change and curse that Posh Girl hasn't included any pennies. My smallest coin is a three-penny bit, and when I'm considering what to do, he says: "that'll do", and takes it. He gives me a friendly wink. I think this is supposed to be my reward for helping him out. I dread what could happen if he rewards those less amenable than me. As it is, I *am* wearing two odd socks, but only grannies and auld dolls can get away with that type of reply. So I'll have to pretend that the threepence with the broken biscuits cost me sixpence.

Leaving the grubbiness of the Tunnel, I head home. I walk through a cluster of trees called the *Plantation* and progress into narrow pathways that cut through the whitewashed housing executive houses of Redville. On my right is a play area called the *Maze*. It's supposed to be a shortcut, but I don't take it in case I get lost. Finally, I pass an electricity pylon. It signals that I'm almost home. I've passed one hundred houses and have seen only three people. Two of them were peering out the window, watching life drift by. The other one was tinkering with a motorbike in his back garden. He had a tattoo. All motorbike freaks have a tattoo.

Around the corner from our house, I am startled by a box of soap powder on the window sill of someone's kitchen. Soap powder doesn't usually surprise me, but this one does. It's OMO soap powder. Boot McConville told me on Thursday that if you see a box of OMO displayed in someone's house, it means *On My Own*. He said that whoever lives there is lookin' for a good ride. I've often noticed the woman who lives in this house. She always wears a short mini skirt that barely covers her ass, exposing her pink polka dot knickers. She's always talking to boys my age and has big diddies. I'm sure that she hasn't seen her toes for years. But that's not what's bothering me. *We* sometimes use OMO in our house, and my ma sometimes keeps it on the kitchen window sill. Our kitchen is at the back of the house, so passers-by wouldn't notice what soap powder we use. But that's not the point. I hurry home, impatient to know what's there. I fiddle with our back gate and glance up at the kitchen window. Thank Christ for that. It's Persil!

Amazingly there's some food in the pan from this morning- a sausage and a bit of potato bread. "Who owns this," I ask my mother.
"Anybody who wants it. You can have it if you want."
She says it generously enough, but something in her tone also suggests she's doing me a favour. It's as if she's saying: N*obody wants it now, but somebody might want it later.*
I turn the gas on.
"I was in Granny McCoubrey's earlier on."
"Anything strange?"
"Aye, there was something strange." I'm laughing aloud.
"What. ...what is it?"
"You don't want to know."

"I do want to know."

"You don't."

"You're starting to get on my nerves. What happened, for God's sake?"

My mouth is full of sausage and potato bread. I point at it and continue chewing. My ma has the dishcloth in her hand. She has stopped washing up to hear my news. I continue chewing past the point where I usually swallow. She's getting agitated.

"Hurry up and swallow whatever's in your mouth. I haven't got all day, ye know."

"Granda McCoubrey pawned the priest's trousers for money to buy drink, and the priest knows about it."

"Jesus, Mary and Saint Joseph. I don't believe ye…you're havin' me on, so ye are."

She looks delighted because she has hit the jackpot with this gossip. It couldn't be juicier if she made it up herself. I relate the whole story, and she makes me repeat it word for word. She now knows more about what happened than I do.

"Wait until your da hears about this. He'll go mad because if there's one thing he hates, it's being shown up. I hope you haven't told anybody else about this, have you? I hope you haven't now."

It's not a question. It's an order.

"What are you doin'?"

"I'm just going to phone our Ita about something."

"You're goin' to phone her about the trousers, aren't you?"

"I've lost her number. Where's the phone book?"

"So it's alright for you to tell people, but it's not alright for me?"

"That's right. Get away from the hall. I don't want people listenin' in on my conversations."

I go into the sitting room instead of going back to the kitchen. This way, I'll be able to hear everything.

In our old house, we weren't allowed into the sitting room. It was for visitors only. The china cabinet was our pride and joy. It was an ornament to be cleaned and polished, kept spick and span for nuns, priests, and particular relatives such as Granny and Granda McWhirter. When our American relatives visited every few years, my mother unlocked the cabinet, and the sitting room was used for sitting. Once they had gone, we were back in the kitchen, all five of us. My Ma always said "No" whenever I asked if I could sit in the sitting room.

"No one's allowed to sit in the sitting room."

One day I asked her if I could *stand in* the sitting room, and she gave me a cuff around the ears. I took that as a "No".

Listening to your provided gossip is just as satisfying as gossiping.

"Don't forget to tell her what Granda said."

The sitting room door is ajar. I'm earwigging her conversation and shouting instructions at the same time. She shoos me away with the back of her hand, but it's half-hearted. She's gibbering delightedly into the phone.

"Tell her the priest was all picture, no sound," I yell. "Tell her."

"He says that the priest was speechless with rage."

Yes! My intervention has worked. I'm part of the gossiping triangle. This is turning into a great day's Saturday.

We'll Support You Evermore

I wash my face, go to the toilet, have a sneaky slug of my da's sarsaparilla, run down the stairs and pat Ben's head on my way out of the front door. Then I open the letterbox and tell him to finish the broken biscuits under my pillow. He tells me he's just had a Pars bun but might eat them later. He'll see. I meet Peter Pope, who's on his way to meet me. Kick-off is in half an hour. "We'd need to get a move on," he says. We stop at a shop called the *Petrol Pump* for sweets. It's a new petrol station that wants to be a supermarket. We buy our Midget Gems and Fanta from a guy with one arm. He's quicker at the till than his two armed colleagues. The man in the queue ahead of us has just bought a box of soap powder. OMO! This guy *does* live on his own, but the only ride I imagine him gettin' is one on his rusty old bicycle.

Portstown supporters are a funny lot. Because our team is very average, the supporters don't have much to cheer about. So instead, they go to home games *expecting* defeat, and when it happens, they criticise their own players. Today is the last game of the season. If their opponents –Glentoran-win, they'll become the Irish league champions.
"Well, Kuri, what do you reckon about the game?"
Pope sometimes calls me Kuri instead of Barry-Joe or McCoubrey. Two years ago, it was Illya Kuryakin. Then it became just Kuryakin, and now it's Kuri. I'm worried that it will soon become K and then disappear completely.
"We've no chance. Portstown are cat, and most of our players are cat except for the goalie and Connolly."
"The goalie's cat too, Kuri."
"Connolly's good. He's our only hope. Here, give us one of those Midget Gems."
"What's wrong with your Midget Gems?"

"I haven't opened them yet. I'll give you some later."

We pass Pope's school, Brownsville Junior High School.

"What's it like in there?"

"It's cat."

"What are the teachers like?"

"Cat."

As we reach Shamrock Showgrounds, we are confronted by a mass of black and white scarves and Belfast accents.

"Come on the Glens, come on the Glens".

I'm pretty small for my age, and now I feel both small and insignificant. The last time I felt this was a couple of months ago when I watched Northern Ireland play Cyprus at Windsor Park Belfast. At half time five or six girls in Dr Martens and tartan trousers noticed that I was wearing a school blazer with *St. Michaels* emblazoned across a green, white, and gold badge. St Michaels is my new school from this September, and my ma had got an excellent second-hand bargain with the blazer. I didn't think that anybody would notice in the dark. However, they started to nudge each other, and one turned round, then another. I watched helplessly as I became the focus of attention. One of them was chewing gum. Another one had a Union Jack tattooed on the back of her hand. She looked like a Russian shot putter. They were all wearing identical bomber jackets. Finally, an ugly, skinny one leered at me and announced in a coarse and aggressive Belfast accent: "At least Georgie Best's a Protestant."

At least twenty-five spectators heard the comment and were sufficiently distracted from the action on the pitch to stare towards the voice. My legs turned to jelly, and I made a pathetic attempt to look around to divert attention from myself. That made it worse. The stares persisted, and I prayed Best would score a goal to save my skin. I was petrified and sick. I couldn't have felt more like a marked man if I had been playing. I could feel my body shrinking, and I felt so small that I could've walked out under the turnstiles. Although I was with two chums, I knew that it was *me* who had been targeted. I waited for the Russian shot putter to throw a punch or the cowardly skinny one to give her Dr Martens some practice. My teeth bounced up and down like Tommy James's piano, clattering uncontrollably into each other. Then my whimpering prayers were answered. George Best *did* score a goal. The posse erupted, and before the celebrations subsided, we slithered away to a more obscure part of the ground. The skinny bitch noticed us and mouthed something. Since we couldn't hear her above the din, she gave us the ups with her two fingers. I could still feel her on my back as we edged away.

"Up yours, too, with bells on it," I thought. "You fuckin' orange bitch."

"Come on, the Glens."

At the entrance, Pope asks a man he knows to lift him over the turnstiles so he doesn't have to pay. I recognise the man's Protestant face. In Portstown, we are born with recognition. The man obliges. Pope is well-built for his age, and it's a bit of a struggle. "I'll see ye in a minute," he shouts from inside the ground. I'm slimmer than Pope, but he's got no shame, and I have. I'm embarrassed to ask anyone to lift me over the stalls because of my age. I'm almost a teenager, for God's sake. What happens if I ask someone and they refuse? Or tell me to piss off! I consider *crawling* under, but there's a chance that I might get trapped beneath the turnstiles. Typical! Too old to go *over* and too old to go *under*. Twelve is a tricky age. It seems that I'm stuck in the middle of everything. I reluctantly pay one shilling for my match ticket and go through.

We huddle among thirty or forty teenage Portstown supporters, all adorned in red and white scarves. The Portstown team's skip is the same colour as Manchester United's. Nothing else is similar. As the players come out, half a dozen children rush onto the pitch with their autograph books and pens. One guy is a fourteen-year-old who I recognise - Rory Rodgers. He still wears short trousers to school, but his mammy allows him to wear long ones at weekends. They are corduroys, not jeans.

I ran onto the pitch last year with a pencil and paper. Every time I approached one of the players, another few youngsters got there before me, so I ran around like a headless chicken. To make matters worse, I dropped my pencil and jotter in a patch of mud. The only free player I could find was our goalie. He was delighted to get some glory, but the lead in my pencil broke as he was scribbling his autograph. His name was Sammy Cowan, but when I looked at my mud-splattered jotter, all I could see was Sammy *Cow.*

"That'll do ok," I told him. "It's better than nothing."

I walked off sheepishly, knowing I'd never go autograph hunting again.

"Come on, the Ports. Come on, the Ports. Come on, the Ports."

"Come on the Glens, Come on the Glens, Come on the Glens."

We're outnumbered two to one in our ground. Kick-off! Within five minutes, Portstown are one nil up. It's a brilliant twenty-five-yard shot from Jimmy Connolly, the player-manager. Ten minutes later, it's two nil. The home supporters can't believe what's happenin'. We last scored two goals in a game two months ago. The red and white scarves fly high, and Glen's supporters are silent.

"We want three, we want three," chant the home fans.

I glance at Pope. He's rubbing his hands gleefully and chanting with the crowd. "We want three. We want three."

He winks at me as if saying: "We've got this one sewn up." I'm nervous. I'd also like *three,* but I don't want the Glens to get *one.* I focus on the pitch, watching for mistakes that might let Glentoran score. I don't understand football supporters who get carried away when their team scores. They start singing and hugging and don't seem worried that the other team might equalise. They think that the game is over once their team has scored.

I see that the Portstown players also seem to think that the game's over. They're getting sloppy in their play. Am I the only one noticing this? The crowd are singing a new song.

"We're on our way to victory.

We shall not be moved.

We're on our way to victory..."

Glentoran score. The singing fizzles out. It recommences but dies of a sudden heart attack ten minutes later when Glentoran equalise. I feel sick because I know this game has only one outcome. Half-time brings some temporary relief. Some men scurry off to the social club while others urinate behind the grandstand. Michael Mackie goes there sometimes! Pope and I relieve ourselves and then share our Midget Gems. He offers me a bite of his *Mars Bar*, but I refuse because he has already eaten a chunk.

"What do you reckon about the second half," I ask Pope.

"I don't know. It hasn't started yet," he replies.

"Very funny, Popey."

I hate when people try to be witty but don't quite manage it. It's nothing personal against Pope because I do it myself. The difference is I realise when I'm not being funny, and they don't.

Second half! Straight from the kick-off, a bespectacled Glentoran player called Bimbo Weathercock lobs the ball over Sammy Cowan and into the empty net. 3-2 to the Glens. They know how to hit the back of the onion bag, which wins football games. The Portstown crowd turn nasty. The small bunch of scarf-wearing supporters beside us start to sing: *The Sash My Father Wore*. I recognise it as the national anthem of Orangemen. It celebrates the victory of Protestant King Billy over Catholic James the Second at the Battle of the Boyne in the seventeenth century. I wonder how this is goin' to help the Portstown forwards hit the onion bag. Pope is singing his heart out. When he sees me, he continues as if I'm not there. I realise that for Pope, I'm *not* there.

At 4-2, it gets worse. The crowd turn nasty on our best player,

Jimmy Connolly. They call him a *Fenian* bastard when he misses a half chance. Good job it wasn't an absolute sitter! He can hear them but keeps the poise of a proud peacock. The songs become vile. One has as its chorus: *Fuck the Pope and the Virgin Mary*. Pope refrains from this one. I can't determine whether he's shocked or just takin' it personally. The game finishes 5-2. Glentoran are the champions, and Portstown are the losers yet again.

We slump out of the ground. On the way home, we pass buses full of Glentoran supporters. They are rubbing our noses in it.
"Portiestown's a nice wee town, but the smell of pigs would knock you down."
Their joy compounds our misery. "Right," says Pope. "When we get to the last bus, we'll grab a scarf each and run like fuck. We'll take the shortcut at the back of the Metal Box."
I see in his face that he means it. There is something carefree about how Protestant boys like Pope swear. The words come out naturally. There are no moral dilemmas, no conscience pricks, and no worrying about having to confess it later to a priest. I don't imagine Pope would be too bothered if his parents heard him swearing like this. It makes me feel a bit jealous.
"If they catch us, we'll be slaughtered...I hope you realise that."
"They won't see us for dust Kuri."
"What happens if the Metal Box gate isn't open?"
"Then we'll climb over the fuckin' thing."
I stare at Pope and hope he's better at climbing gates than clambering over turnstiles. Adrenalin starts to invade my body, and I know that we're going through with it.

"We are the champions. We are the champions."
The Glentoran buses are bouncing with joy. Dangling outside are scores of triumphant black and white scarves. Their owners are waving some of them. Others have been hung out of the bus and clamped from inside using the roll-up windows. Pope grabs one of these, but it's stuck. He swings on it, and it rips apart. He has three feet of the scarf in his hands, but the remaining

nine inches of black and white cloth clings onto the top of the window. Glentoran supporters are mouthing obscenities at us. One of them looks like a hateful thug. As he concentrates on us, I focus on the scarf he's clutching and shaking viciously. It's dangling outside at an inviting height. So the instant the snake inside the bus catches me with the hiss of his eyes, I accept the invitation. Galvanised by the picture of savagery on his face, I snatch at his scarf. My adrenalin surges when I see it in my hands. All of it! Not a tattered one, as Pope has grabbed. I fly along the footpath as people come flooding out of the bus and reach the Metal Box gate just as Pope vaults over its rim.

I know they'll never catch us now, but we still run for our lives. A hundred yards later, we are on top of a hilly ridge and can chance a look back. We see a few Glentoran supporters in the field beside the gate. They're calling us all the names under the Portstown sun. Maybe they think that by shouting louder, they'll get their scarves back. They're wrong. We stretch our trophies above our heads. Then we chant in unison: "We are the champions, we are the champions." Verbal missiles scream towards us. We return fire by hoisting our black and white scarves even higher. My shoes and trousers are plastered in muck, but I don't give a damn. I feel elated and victorious.

The shortcut leads us back to the Petrol Pump shop. We celebrate with a quarter of Wine Gums. They feel more grown up than Midget Gems and deserve our mouths. The one-armed bandit is still serving. *Does he ever take a break, even to go to the toilet?* He's wearing the same black woollen jumper that he wears every day. The sleeve that covers his stump hangs limply like an unfilled Christmas stocking. He must be hot today. I observe it and am reminded of the cloth remnant that is Pope's new scarf.
"Hi Popey, do you think they're still flying that bit of scarf out of the bus?"
"There's not too much left of it now."
He laughs loudly. "They could always keep it and give it to one of

their dwarf supporters," he shouts.

"What are ye on about?"

"You won't believe me, but I saw a dwarf supportin' Glentoran today. At first, I thought it was a child with his da, but when he turned round, he had a beard."

"Does that mean he didn't have a beard *before* he turned round?"

"Don't be stupid, McCoubrey. Do you think he just grew one in about ten minutes?"

"He might have. Was he wearin' trousers?"

"No, he was wearin' a skirt…what do ye think he was wearin' ye head case?"

"I just thought he might be wearin' turn-ups in his underpants instead."

Pope laughs, and a wine gum falls out of his mouth.

"Turn-ups in his underpants! Where did ye hear that one?"

He slaps me heavily on the back as if to congratulate me. It's a bit too heavy, but I don't mind. Pope's in stitches and is zigzagging all over the footpath. He's wearing his stolen scarf. I'm laughing just as much but keep a straight line. I put *my* scarf on.

"I wonder if that wee dwarf is wearing his scarf now," I shout.

"Who, Jimmy Clitheroe?"

Now we're both zigzagging.

"Aye, Jimmy Clitheroe."

I'm still disappointed with the result.

"You know Popey; if Portstown had held on to the two-nil lead until halftime, they might have won that game. If that useless goalkeeper of ours had saved that shot from Bimbo Weathercock, and if Fleming hadn't fouled their player for the second goal, we could easily have won that game. I'm telling ye."

"And if your aunty had balls, she'd be your uncle."

I'm startled by this comment; it takes a while to digest it. When I do, I'm choking on my Wine Gum. I imagine my Aunty Aileen with balls. It doesn't work. She's still my Aunty Aileen. I try again, but all I can picture is Uncle Aileen. Uncle Aileen looks exactly like Aunty Aileen. I realise that there's *only one* Aunty

Aileen, and imagine myself back at the Shamrock Showgrounds with a thousand people singing:
"There's only one, Aunty Aileen. There's only one, Aunty Aileen. One, Aunty Aileen. There's only one, Aunty Aileen."
I see a smiling woman who likes *Big Tom and the Mainliners*. Now I know what Pope meant.

The pan is still on the cooker. The scent of fresh bacon wafts through the kitchen. I hope that I'm included. We know someone who works at Denny's, and we get a sizeable white packet of bacon delivered every weekend. I'm unsure of the payment arrangements because I never see money changing hands. Maybe my da pays in the pub, or it's a gift. It must come cheap because my mother never complains when she catches me frying some. If she sees me taking a slug of milk, it's a bawling match, though I think that's as much about bad manners as it is about penny-watching. I've noticed that she never protests when my father licks his plate. I think that's about fear.

McCoubrey is reading the sports results.
"Glentoran 5, Portstown 2".
There's something eerie about hearing the result of a game you were at an hour ago, especially when your team lost. It's not a secret any more. The whole bloody country knows now. I like McCoubrey, but he uses a mocking tone when mediocre teams like Portstown lose.
"Glentoran 5." Pause, followed by a rueful smile and a wee twinkle in the eye. "Portstown 2."
He says "2" in a deliberate way. There's a bit of the: *better luck next time, but you'll need it because, let's face it, you're crap* tone. It's a bit too sincere to be construed as sarcasm, according to my mother's definition, but it contains a little jibe. I know McCoubrey's game because I can read him like a book. *He's mocking us; that's what he's doin'. I hope you don't think you're being witty, McCoubrey. I hope you don't.*

Saturday Night

They're going out tonight. My mother has her curlers in. Lona has helped her by spending part of the afternoon finding the nits in her hair. I used to do this job but felt it was girl's work. It was too much effort for a measly sixpence. As she moves about the kitchen, the varicose veins on the back of her legs attract me. They look like two streaks of blue lightning. I wince in pity. She doesn't deserve this - scars caused by running around after the likes of me. I make sure that she doesn't catch me lookin' at her. My only escape is to leave the room and go to the toilet for an unneeded piss. I splash water over my face but can't erase the image. I'm still seeing blue.

When I go downstairs, my mother says: "What about a wee cup of tea?" She's not looking at anyone in particular, but I know she's asking me. It's an order. She hasn't put her make-up on yet, but there's always time for tea. I'm chokin' for a cup myself, so I go to the kitchen and make it. This way, it won't be milky, and the cup will be full. Just as the teapot comes to the boil, the doorbell rings. I turn off the gas knob and rush to the door. I know it's not Popey because it's tea time. It doesn't take long to see the silhouette of one of the neighbours from across the street, Sharon Hobsbawn. I know what she wants, but I decide to make her sweat.
"Hi ya, Sharon."
I'm about to ask if there's anything that I can do for her. I realise this is too much of an invitation, so I merely smile. She smiles back. It's a knowing look, but tonight I don't know anything. Portstown lost, didn't they?

Her pale freckly face reddens. I like that.
"Is it ok if I use your phone….I won't be long?"
The last time she said that she was here for half an hour. I smirk wryly, hoping that it registers. Then I nod her in towards

the hall, leaving her standing at the glass semi-circular phone table. I shut the sitting room and kitchen doors so she has some privacy. I'm pretty considerate about such things, especially for strangers.

"Who is it," whispers my mother.

"Who do you think?" I reply as I turn the TV up.

"That's too loud, Barry-Joe."

I put my index finger to my lips and whisper in her ear.

"I don't want her to know we're listenin' to her conversation."

My mother nods in agreement.

"Turn it down a wee bit anyway," she says.

I'm stuffing custard creams into my mouth. I have the TV to myself, a full cup of strong tea on the floor, and thoughts from today in my head. I laugh aloud as I replay the scarf incident repeatedly in my mind. A shiver of excitement vibrates through my body. If they had caught me, I would have been lynched. Grown men would have stamped on my head and made mincemeat out of me. I feel a brogue slamming against my ribs, and I shudder. Time for another custard cream!

My da waits on my ma to get ready. When he notices her cup of tea on the mantelpiece, he stares long and hard at it. He glances at his watch, comparing its time with the fireplace clock. His uncle gave him the Swiss gold watch before he died. Da's freshly shaven face does it justice. I notice he looks younger when he shaves, even though his head's as bald as a baby's bum. I don't know why he bothers with his parting since only a few tufts of hair remain on top. On the other hand, I don't want him to look like those men with *no* parting. Nor the ones who part their hair half an inch above the ear. No way! My da's still not a bad-lookin' man. His neat moustache deflects attention from his baldy head. It has grey flecks, but it makes him look distinguished. Looking distinguished might be one rung below being good-looking, but it's two rungs higher than a parting beside your left ear.

He sends me out for the evening sports paper, **Ireland's**

Saturday Night. On the way home, I have an impulse to collect cigarette butts that passers-by discard. A guy aged about twenty nonchalantly tosses one. He flicks it over the bonnet of someone's car. I search it out. Bingo! He's left half the cigarette. I hastily scan the road for somewhere to put it and soon find an empty twenty packet of Embassy. Feeling elated, I slip the smouldering cigarette inside. I spot an old guy going in the opposite direction. Since he's smoking, I'm going that way too. I linger behind until he eventually discards his fag. Pretending to tie my shoelaces, I examine my catch. It's a Woodbine and has been smoked to a tiny butt. Stingy git! I hope you burnt your fingers. Still, something's better than nothing, so I throw it into the box. It falls to the bottom corner, barely breathing smoke. Within half an hour, my box is full, and I'm outside the house, planning my entrance. A dozen butts are smoking in my cigarette packet. Soon I'll savour each one. Sharon Hobsbawn is walking away from our house. She's tall and gangly. She said she wouldn't be long and look at the length of her!

I give my da the paper and all his change. He checks it and gives me a shilling. I grunt and disappear to the bathroom that my mother has amazingly vacated. Locking the door, I anxiously wait for them to go out. I'm trembling, so I decide to compose myself with a smoke. I put the hot cigarette box on the edge of the sink. Then I shake it, hoping for one of the sizeable filtered butts to emerge. Instead, the scrawny Woodbine falls out. Its ash tip hits the sink and turns a damp shade of black. I manage to pick it up and puff like billio. I've never been taught the kiss of life, but I'm sure this is it. I suck and blow until I'm exhausted but can't see any smoke. There *isn't* any smoke. The *Woodbine* butt is a goner. When I hear a loud bang on the door, I realise I'm a goner too.

"What the hell's goin' on in here"?
I recoil and almost fall into the pot. The smouldering cigarette packet falls from my hand, and various butts spill onto the cold

oilcloth floor. I cover up, waiting for fist blows or a right boot into my thigh. Instead, he raises his right arm aggressively, and I experience that momentary breathing space that occurs before someone smacks you. But the onslaught doesn't arrive. So I bravely peep through my clenched elbows and see my da glaring in disgust. I'm speechless, knocked back by his leering stare and feeling the weight of his disdain. Pathetically, I loosen my arms and gaze at the floor. I feel so low that I could flush myself down the toilet if I was sure I'd emerge at the other end.

"You're not worth the effort. Did you ever hear of germs and diseases? If you want a cigarette, I'll give you one that no filthy person has sucked, and you can puff at it until your heart's content. What the friggin' hell possessed you to pick up other people's leftovers? I thought you had more bloody sense."

It feels like a slow dagger through my heart because I thought I *had* more bloody sense. I have more sense, but I don't know why I did it. "Never again," I tell myself, and then aloud: "It won't happen again." The shame of having to apologise is unbearable. I'm not used to having proper conversations with any of my parents, and it feels like I'm virtually apologising for existing, for being born. He disappears, and I hear myself breathing deeply, my first proper breath for five minutes. I gather the butts and flush them down the toilet in disgust. One refuses to go and stubbornly bobbles on the water. A second flush drowns it. I stay upstairs until they leave. The back door slams shut with a certainty that convinces me they've gone. It's an angry exit. Then the wooden gate clicks and I watch them get into the car. Nothing happens for a minute or so. Even though we live in a cul-de-sac, he constantly checks the back mirror. Finally, when I peep through the net curtains again, I glimpse our car disappearing from view, driven by a man with a shiny bald head. Now it's safe for me to go downstairs.

I linger at the window that overlooks the car park behind our house. A small child is standing on the opposite pavement, wearing a *Slappy Joe* and a nappy. He seems content enough, though he must be cold. Perhaps he's contemplating what he's let himself in for, being born in a place like this with no sinner in sight. His mother appears and disturbs him, but he doesn't budge. Instead, he stares at the road when she lifts him as if he's spotted something interesting. I avert my gaze to the top of our coal shed and am intrigued by an elegant high heel shoe standing upright near the apex. It has no scuff marks or apparent blemishes. Nor has it a match.

Aunty Aileen has cancelled my babysitting as I knew she would. She's found a real babysitter. It's all over the head of her that I've been caught with the butts. If she hadn't cancelled, everything would've been dandy. Young people in Portstown stay at home on Saturday nights. My highlight is the Val Doonican show. Val wears a new jumper weekly and talks about it for fifteen minutes. Then he plays his guitar and sings ballads. The other boys in my class claim to hate Val, but his songs bring tears to my eyes, even when he's singing about *Delaney's Donkey, especially* when he's singing about *Delaney's Donkey*! I'm envious of his cleanliness and his big fluffy coloured sweaters. These are signs of his success as a singer, and I'm jealous of successful people. *They* don't have to live in a shithole like Portstown. Behind Doonican's cosy smile sits a businessman. He's doing it for the money, not for love.

I can see through you, Val. Don't think I can't. All you smiling Irish Free Staters, trying to ingratiate yourselves to the English with your supposed charm and lovely brogue. Lovely brogue, my ass! There's another man called Wogan, a radio DJ doing the same brogue thing. Why can't he stay in Ireland and get a job in the bank instead of coming across the airwaves with this plastic mid-Atlantic accent? He's from Limerick, for God's sake, home of the bog men. It would be ok for me to become famous in England because I'm from Northern Ireland, part of Britain. If they own my country, then I'm entitled to get famous over there. More than Val Doonican or Terry Wogan, that's for sure.

Sunday Morning

He's coughing and spluttering downstairs as he makes breakfast. It's his penance for getting a bit drunk last night and a chance for my ma to have a rare lie-in. The smell of the frying pan arouses me, but I don't want to get up too soon. Timing is everything in these situations. Give him time to cook the fry-up. Don't disturb him while he's busy. I feel guilty that he has to work all week and cook breakfast, but the feeling lasts no more than three seconds. He's the adult, and I'm not a teenager yet. After all, it's his responsibility, not mine.

"So you decided to get up?" (*Mmmh. What does it look like.....does it look like I'm still in bed?*)
"There's a bit of soda bread and bacon and egg in the pan—you'd better hurry up before the rest of them get up."
I help myself, and he observes. I don't take as much as I'd like to since the last thing I want is another bollocking after last night. I return a bit of fried scrambled egg into the pan. This gesture is *my* penance for the weekend. I'm living in a house full of sinners.

I check the clock to ensure it's at least one hour until mass time. Otherwise, I won't be able to eat *anything*. I've got ten minutes to spare, and that's plenty as I'm still learning the meaning of the word *chew*. I get exasperated when I'm sitting opposite someone who's chewing slowly. Don't they understand the function of their Adam's apple? When you think they're about to swallow or *have* swallowed, their jaws start circling like billio. It doesn't bother me if it's someone my age, but if it's an adult like my Aunty Ita, it's purgatory. It becomes a competition to see who can eat the slowest, which causes a massive problem for someone like me because I hate losing and eating slowly. So we sit eyeballing each other, her pretending that she eats like this in her own house and me pretending that I do likewise at home. She wears that sneaky smile that people use when they're playing games with ye, games you're not supposed to win. Sometimes it gets so ridiculous that she pretends that she *has* swallowed, and when I stupidly follow suit, she stares blankly at me, and a big bulge appears in the corner of her mouth. Then, I hear her chewing again, a bit louder than before. At that moment, I know the game's over. You lost again, McCoubrey. You lost.

Lona refuses to give me one of her Love hearts. I want a love heart, and there's a limit to how long I can watch her stuff them into her gob, one after the other.
"Give me one of them, will ye, for God's sake."
"Wait, and I will."
"I won't wait all day. You're starting to get on my nerves."
"And you're starting to get on my goat."
"Stick it up your bum."
"I will then, so I will."
"I'm warning you now."
"What do ye mean you're warning me? They're not your sweets are they?"
"This is your last chance. If you don't give me a Love Heart this minute, I'll eat the whole packet on ye."
"If you do, I'll tell my da."
"You can tell whoever you want. Just give me one."
"No."
She sets another one onto her stretched tongue and swivels it into her mouth. No smile, just an act of defiance.

"That's it."
I dive towards her and try to prise the packet of sweets from her hand. She has anticipated this, and her hand is now a fist. I grab it and twist. No joy. I dig my nails into her veins and nip her viciously, so hard that I instantly know I've been too brutal.

She shrieks as the little packet of plastic cracks onto the tiled floor. We both dive at it. I manage to smother them before Lona crumples on top of me, screaming with pain at her loss. I can't contain my laughter. To the victor, the spoils: the Love Hearts are mine. I'm overjoyed at my victory, and the more she screams, the more I tremble with the excitement of it all. My being older and bigger than her is irrelevant. If Lona were a baby in a pram, I'd still be thrilled at the outcome.

My right ear smarts instantly as something whacks it. It's someone's hand. This isn't a mere cuff on the side of the jaw. It's grievous bodily harm. I sprawl toward the fireplace, and as I'm about to look up, I see my father's boot flying towards my belly. It doesn't match the one on the coal shed roof. Too shiny and new. It's hard-wearing though, because it stuns and propels me forward. My head twists in a mid-air spin and ricochets off the corner of the fireplace as the rest of me slumps onto its base, bum first. If my head were a ball, it would be like hitting it against the crossbar at speed and seeing it bounce over the line. My da has scored alright. *GOALLLLLLLLLLLLLLLLLLL!* Blood is gushing down my face, warm and red. *Nice shot there, da, an absolute peach of a shot. A wee bit of leftovers there from last night, eh? Fuuuuuggggggghhhhhh!*

"It serves you damn rightly... that's what you get for pickin' on someone half your age. You wouldn't let it go, would ye? I heard ye from out there in the kitchen, tormentin' her all over a bloody sweet. If you're bleedin', it's your own bloody fault. It's all over the head of you that you hit your head against the bloody fireplace. It wouldn't have happened if you hadn't been tormentin' the child."

The only thing over my head is blood, lots of it. My hand is slapped tight against the place where I feel the wound, and still the red stuff dribbles through it. I'm afraid to remove it in case the dribble becomes a gush. My da has left the room to go into the kitchen, and I'm standing there helpless, staring at Lona neutrally. I'm not angry at her. Indeed I would welcome any helpful advice about what I should do next.

"Get me a piece of toilet roll, will ye."

She scampers off and returns seconds later with a foot of paper. It's that tracing paper shit that we use in school. It might be suitable for drawing, but it's useless for wiping your ass or soaking up blood. It's 1971, for Christ's sake. Is the McCoubrey family so poor that we can't afford the bog roll with the blotting paper texture that soaks everything up, including blood? My blood is sliding along this cheap stuff and dripping onto the floor. I'm suddenly aware that I'm panicking because I'm scared. Then my mother appears, holding a damp face cloth.

"What kept you? I've been like this for ten minutes."

"Don't exaggerate. I'm not at your beck and call, and I've only one pair of hands, ye know. I'm not a bloody octopus, so I'm not."

"I didn't say you were."

"Shut up and let me have a look."

I freeze so that she can assess the damage.

"For cryin' out loud, how the hell did you manage to do this?"

"It wasn't my fault."

"It wasn't my fault either," says Lona. "Daddy kicked him for stealin' my sweets, and he hit his head against the bloomin' fireplace."

"Yous aren't even supposed to be in this room anyway. It's the sittin' room, not the fightin' room."

"Is it deep?"

"Shut up and stand still until I see what I'm doin'."

She stares intently into my hair and presses on my skull.

"AAAGGGHHHHA."

"You're going to need stitches. Could you not have picked another day except Sunday for this to happen?"

I process this for the future and remain still as her examination continues.

"Does it need stitches?"

"Yes."

"How many?"

"I'm not a friggin' doctor, ye know… Lona, tell your da to come here a minute."

You'd think that *he* was a friggin' doctor.

He enters the sitting room as if inspecting an accident that has nothing to do with him.

"Let me see."

I turn my head obediently towards him. He grips it firmly and peers at my cut.

"I'll take him down to McInally, and we can go to 11.30 mass. Has anybody rang the doctor yet?"

"I'll ring him now," says my ma. "Here, Lona, go and get me a small towel, will ye."

I'm trying to think of any *big* towels in the house. The tracing paper is on the sitting room floor, and the green face cloth is red.

"Go and wash your face before we go," says my da.

I examine the dyed facecloth. I hope he's not thinking what I'm thinking.

We walk the whole way to the doctor's surgery. My da steps briskly in front, and I trot behind, with the towel pressed tightly against my skull. I'm terrified of slackening it even a tiny bit in case I lose a pint of blood. The farther we go, the quicker I have to run to keep up. I want to tell him to slow down, but he's the man, and I'm the boy. The doctor's surgery is in a large townhouse opposite the Protestant church. We wait an eternity after ringing the bell. Eventually, an old guy in braces cautiously opens the door. His mouth has bits of yellow stuck to it, and I smell the waft from a frying pan. Now I know why he took his time. He listens as my father explains the cause of my blood.

"He tripped backwards over the mantelpiece and took a bit of a knock."

The doctor looks at me for confirmation.

"I don't know how it happened. One minute I was standin' in the sittin' room, and the next, I fell against the fireplace. I tried to protect my face but hit my head instead. It was an accident. It was my own fault."

I've always been taught not to tell tales and am aware of the impact of my own words. My father's face remains neutral, but I can sense the acknowledgement deep within his eyes. I'm pleased with how I'm conducting myself, but part of me wants to shout, *ACCIDENT, MY ASS*. Instead, I shut up while the old guy examines my head. His grip is firm. He dabs my wound with a damp cloth and gets me to press down on it. Glancing at his watch, he mutters something about stitches without a freeze. I think he might be worried that his tea's getting cold.

"You might feel a wee bit sore with these stitches, son, but you'll be all right."

I can see a thick black thread dangling by his side, which has appeared from nowhere. He cleans my blood again and goes to work. The pain is sharp and penetrating. I grit my teeth and gasp for breath between each stitch. He stitches me three times without saying a word. When it's over, I stand alone in the cold hall while my da pays him.

"I thought doctors were free?" I ask my da when we're outside.

"Not on Sundays, they're not," he replies. "And certainly not this one."

11.30 MASS in Portstown is the dreaded one. It's the same as winning the booby prize on Take Your Pick. Father Quinlan is the regular priest for this slot, and his sermons are all fire and brimstone. Today is no different. He's talking about the scourge of alcohol.

"Men who drink too much, come home drunk on Friday night without the family wages, and neglect their family duties by getting drunk… should hang their head in shame. If there are any such sinners here today, and I have noticed a few, you should hang your heads in shame and ask God for his forgiveness."

I peer through my sweaty hands and notice that the congregation has their heads hung low. Are they all alcoholics?

Quinlan's on a roll, and his face is purple. "I hear some men drink 4, 5, 6, or even 7 pints of beer in one night. What do you call that?" Silence. "What do you call that?" He surveys the crowd. Is he looking for a reply? No one else is allowed to talk except the man in the pulpit, for God's sake. A man stands up in front of me. He must be brave to leave in the middle of Quinlan's sermon. But he's not going. Instead, he stares straight at the pulpit.

"Ye call that getting drunk, Father? Well, you can add a few more pints of beer onto your 6 or 7. 9 or 10's more likely, and then a couple of shots of whisky, and then you're ready for the road… the rocky road to Dublin … and that's exactly where I'm headed this minute."

It's Mr Kielty from my estate, still drunk from last night. He's a good friend of my granda. He stumbles out from the middle of the row. People make way for him as if he's a leper. Some are sniggering. Others are stunned. Kielty looks serious. I watch his solemn face and see a smirk of disgust. This man might be drunk, but something is bothering him. You can see he doesn't have much time for religion or priests. So what's he doing here in that case? I'm sure he's been barred from a few pubs, but he's about to become the first person in Portstown banned from the chapel. Of course, they'll ridicule and scoff at him, but there's something about his behaviour that I secretly admire.

I'm obliged to take Holy Communion with my stitched-up head. On the way up the aisle, I hang *my* head in shame in case anyone sees my cut. I like to be anonymous when queuing up for communion, but that's impossible in Portstown. Hoping the congregation won't gape at you is like asking the hunchback of Notre Dame to straighten up or the Elephant Man to smile. I can feel the stares on the back of my head. They zoom in on my stitches, and I'm convinced everyone knows the story of the fireplace and my da's right boot. Today's bonus time for them - a drunken rant and a boy with a hole in his head. Kielty and I have provided them with their Sunday helpings of gossip. It'll tide them over until something more interesting comes their way. As the communion wafer melts in my mouth, I realise I'm an extra in a religious soap opera I don't want to be in. The straightjacket of religion is squeezing my life out and turning me into a bloomin' sheep. If I have to be a sheep, I'd rather be a black one like Kielty! *Baa, Baa, Baa,……Baa!*

We go to Granny McWhirter's afterwards. I can smell boiling cabbage. It's been on the stove since 9 o'clock this morning. She's fiddling about in the kitchen, preparing to cook the stewing meat. My granda squints at me.

"What's that on your head? It looks like stitches or something?"

"It *is* stitches."

"Dear God, what happened to you?"

"I fell against the fireplace."

"How did you do that?"

"I don't know. I just lost my balance, so I did."

"Did you go to the doctor?"

"Aye."

"Who, Dr McInally?"

"Yeah."

"You're lucky he was opened on Sunday. I say, Danny, you're lucky McInally was there of a Sunday. He's the type of doctor that suits himself, so he does."

My da nods.

"I think they have to have somebody available for emergencies, Barney…..and they charge the emergency rate as well, I can tell ye."

"Is that right? They must be on double time or something."

"You can say that again."

And he does.

"Aye, they must be on double time or something Danny, the same as the building sites. When I was a crane driver, they'd pay us time and a half on a Saturday and double time for Sundays, but it was rare to get work on a Sunday. Too dear for them, I suppose."

My granny appears from the scullery.

"Hi ya, Barry-Joe and Danny. Let me see your cut."

She gapes at my skull for about three minutes and then says: "It's terrible too".

She disappears into the scullery. I can hear her rummaging around in a hidden cupboard. Finally, she returns with a large white bag of sweets.

"Here you are, have a sweet."

 I dip my hand in.

"Take two if you want."

I drop the one squashed between my thumb and the palm of my hand and extract two hard-boiled sweets. She then gives one to my da, and we all sit sucking sweets. Finally, my da picks up the Sunday Independent and turns to the sports pages. Granda McWhirter excuses himself.

"I've just got to finish polishing the car."

It's a 1966 Ford Anglia, and the plastic is still on the seats. It's the newest-looking car in Portstown, and he only drives it as a last resort. So when he shines it up, you can see your reflection better than in any mirror.

My granny also excuses herself. She goes and scrubs the front doorway until the white semi-circle of cleanliness is whiter. I sit alone with my da while he checks his losers from yesterday's horseracing. Why does he have to suck his sweet so friggin' loud? I lose patience with mine and bite it into tiny melting pieces. Suddenly he folds his paper noisily and sets it at his side.

"Shall we go?" He's already halfway out of the living room. My granny moves away from the front door.

"Are yous away?"

"Aye, cheerio. We'll see you later."

He steps over the semi-circle, and I jump deliberately over it so my granny can see I've easily missed it.

"Cheerio."

"Bye-bye, son, be careful with your sore head."

I have to run to catch up with my da.

"You could eat your grub off her friggin' doorstep," he mutters.

A trumpet interrupts my Sunday dinner of two cubes of stewing meat, three bits of potato, and some peas. "It's the Salvation Army," shouts my ma. "Where's my purse?" She searches and pulls out five new pence. "This bloody decimal currency is a joke. Has anybody got any *old money*, sixpence, or even a few coppers? I'm not giving them this much, so I'm not." No one replies, so she runs upstairs and returns with some change. "Here, Lona, when they knock on the door, give them this, but don't be entering into any discussions with them. Do you hear me?"

"Yes, I hear you, so I do."

"Good."

I see a set of twins I recognise from the football. The Matchetts! They're cheerleaders for the hundred ardent Portstown fans that are weekly sadists. One is playing the trumpet, the other the trombone. I wonder why they aren't playing the same instrument. But, of course, I can play three notes on the recorder, so I'm not entitled to criticise their musical ability. It's pretty woeful, though. They're all reading something from gigantic pages.

"What are they reading," Lona asks my ma.

"They're reading music."

"Well, they're cat, so they are."

"It's better than nothing, isn't it?"

"No, it's worse than nothing, so it is."

"Just give him the bloomin' money when he calls, will ye."

Lona's right. They must be reading the Sunday Express or the News of the World because the notes are off-key. It's brutal. I turn to my mother.

"Surely you're not going to give them money for *that*?"

"For crying out loud, will ye shut your mouth," she shouts.

I study the twins. One of them is lanky and cheerful. The other is also slim but slightly darker and more handsome. But

I detect sneakiness in his brown beady eyes. Even though he's standing in the middle of the group, he looks like the leader. He's alert and aware of his surroundings. I feel relieved to be inside and wonder if he can see through brick walls. Something tells me that these twins aren't interested in saving anyone but themselves. Their da's a policeman, so maybe they like wearing uniforms. Lona opens the door before the Salvation Army guy arrives. She hands him some change, and he pretends not to count it. "Thanks for your support," he says as Lona closes the door in his face. A minute later, he and his comrades are on the march towards the next street, playing *"How Wonderful Thou Art"*. I'm sure they haven't dedicated it to us.

After dinner, I'm half expecting Popey to knock, but I hope he doesn't. I've noticed that he's been acting a bit strange lately. He seems aloof and preoccupied. He's started hanging around with a few of his schoolmates, even though they don't live in Redville. Sometimes he comes home late, and I spied him from the bus last week with his arm on some boy's shoulder. He was smiling like you do when you're happy – like there's no place you'd rather be. I don't like anyone to touch *my* shoulder or any other part of me. Not even Popey! Indeed, I don't particularly want to see anyone *happy* unless it's my ma or da. Or Lona and young Ben! And they don't count since they're family. What made it even worse was that I recognised his pal. He's the fella who stopped me on my way home from school a month ago and asked me if I was a Fenian. I instinctively knew that he wasn't being friendly. As I don't know the exact meaning of Fenian, I denied it and remember feeling a terrible rush of guilt. He called me a lying Fenian bastard, and I replied meekly: "I'm not lying." I wasn't sure whether I was denying being a Fenian, a bastard or both. He was much bigger than me and looked like he could fight. It was his territory, and the streets were full of Union Jacks. I was scared and tried to walk past him. He shoved me a few times and said: "If I see you around this way again, I'll bust your friggin' jaw, ye Fenian bastard." I've walked home that way a few times since, including the day of the Hot Chocolate, but I don't feel comfortable any more. That's why I'm glad it's the school holidays. I can change my routine and avoid running the gauntlet.

Sunday Afternoon

McGann calls at the door. I wasn't expecting him, but I feel obliged to go out as he has had a long journey to my estate. Plus, I'm not in the mood for Pope today. Although my head's splitting, I fancy being away from my da for a bit. Having time to digest my dinner would have been nice, but I won't tell McGann. I quickly explain the plaster on my eyebrow before he enquires.

"I tripped over the fireplace and banged my head on the mantelpiece."

"Pull the other one. There's bells on it."

"I had to get three stitches ... the friggin' doctor didn't use any freeze, so he didn't."

"Cry me a river McCoubrey, you big pansy."

McGann doesn't delve further, and I'm grateful for that.

We walk together without saying much but know where we're going. When we arrive at the Public Park, the gates are locked. A massive bolt and chain dangle at eye level. We feel it, tug at it, twist it, pull it, kick it and then check again to see if anything has happened. Zilcho! The park gates are locked until whoever controls the keys decides otherwise. We knew this would happen, but sometimes you hope for a miracle. *Keep on hoping, boys, because Portstown is a miracle-free zone. They might happen in Fatima or Lourdes, but not here.*

"Someday we're goin' to come here, McCoubrey and these friggin' gates will be open."

"Catch yourself on."

"I'm serious."

"So am I."

"No, seriously, they can't keep the place locked forever."

"Yes, they can."

"Are you tryin' to tell me that these same gates will be locked if we come back here in ten years' time?"

"You might be comin' back here in ten years' time, but I won't be."

"Aye, but ye know what I mean, stop twistin' things."

"I'm not twistin' anything. I just said I wouldn't be here in ten years' time. I mightn't even be here next week."

"What happens if you're not here next week and the gates are open?"

"Have a titter a wit, will ye."

"But what happens?"

"Are you as thick as Champ or what? You walk in without jumpin' over the gate; that's what happens."

"You're a real smart Alec sometimes, McCoubrey, do ye know that?"

"Are we going to climb over this friggin' thing or not?"

"Come on then."

We go to the play area and head for the swings. I notice a girl called Lucy laughing with a small group of friends. Her hair is long, wavy and auburn. Usually, I don't like reddish hair, but Lucy's isn't too ginger. Plus, she's got big diddies. Lucy excites me. Maybe she doesn't! The chains of the swings are wrapped around its support and padlocked. The wooden seats are suspended four feet off the ground. A dwarf could probably squeeze into the chair and have a mini swing. But, of course, somebody would have to lift him up first. "Christ," says McGann, "the swings are locked." I glare at him. "What did you expect? They've been locked every Sunday for the last year." We pull at the chains and try to untangle them, as I'd love a good swing to rest my sore feet and float free. Five minutes would do. No chance! The damned swings are closed for business today. All I can do is stare at them, just like when window shoppin' after Mass most Sundays. I spend my life wishing that Sunday was Monday. Portstown must be the most hateful town on earth.

We walk a few yards to the see-saw, keeping Lucy and her mates within earshot. McGann hops onto one end, and I clamber cautiously onto the other, ensuring maximum comfort for my crotch. Arms flailing, he starts to bounce up and down. I'm holding on grimly, but I needn't have bothered. The thrill has lasted less than one-tenth of a second. I'm about four inches above base level, facing down slightly towards McGann. This is no good. I should be counting the nits in his hair. My turn to bounce! I jump up and thump my ass downwards onto the damp iron. Ouch! Shit! My feet stay on the potholed tarmac, and McGann laughs at me, his brogues dangling just above the surface.

"What's goin' on?"

"Have a look at the friggin' thing, will ye McCoubrey."

I peer to the side of the see-saw and see a spanking new padlock and chain.

"I don't friggin' believe it…first the swings and now the see-saw… I didn't see that damn thing, did you?"

"If I did, I wouldn't be standin' here, would I?"

"What the hell… it's movin' a bit… I suppose somethin's better than nothin'."

"That's what your ma said to your da last night, McCoubrey."

We both start bouncing up and down gleefully.

"Boy, this is some contraption, McGann. Watch you don't fall off now."

"That's the other thing your ma told your da last night."

I think she's givin' me the eye because I caught her lookin' at me just now. She was watchin' us on the see-saw and then diverted her eyes towards me. We eye each other for a few seconds. I'm first to avert, partly to pretend I'm a bit shy, but I also feel stupid starin' at someone like a dummy. A dummy with a patch on his forehead! She's smiling in my direction. I look deliberately over my shoulder. The coast is clear. There's no way it can be McGann. She's hardly going to fancy a boy who will be baldy when he grows up. Of course, that's presuming that he *does* grow up. I won't say anything to him. Look at the cut of him…still gallopin' away, oblivious to my secret thrill. *You're crafty enough there,*

McCoubrey - sitting where you can see Lucy and McGann can't. There are no flies on you, boy. You're a sneaky git, so you are. Aren't you? Maybe I'm not!
"Giddy-up there, boy, giddy-up."
"Your head's cut, McCoubrey," shouts McGann.
"You think so, do ye?"

We wander over to the paddling pool. It's not locked, but it might as well be. It's as dry as a bone apart from a few dank rainwater puddles. No swings, no seesaw and no friggin' water! This is a great park altogether. There's a game in progress on the football pitch, so we head that way. We pass by the duck pond. It used to be thirty yards in diameter and full of ducks and geese. But the authorities have recently started filling it in with soil, and now it's the size of my granny's scullery. Only two ducks remain, bobbing up and down on dirty water less than a foot deep. I hope they know how to fly.

The game's about twenty a side. Most players are Tunnel boys who have sneaked through a hole in the park perimeter wire fence. No clambering over iron gates for these guys. *Lucky Ducks…so long as they don't go near the pond.* A few of the men are wearing Celtic tops over their jeans. One person is kitted out properly- top, shorts, socks, football boots, shin pads, the whole heap. I study him. *He's* got ginger hair. I wonder if he's related to Lucy. He's useless. Just now, he tried to head the ball but blinked instead. It has bounced off his shoulder and is rolling towards the corner flag. Somebody shouts: "Hard lines Bimbo… keep your head up now." I can't work out whether they're trying to cheer him up or give instructions.

A guy called Wishy runs over to the sidelines and taps someone for a fag. He has a few drags and walks back onto the pitch, clutching his butt. Everyone's chasing the ball. Ninety per cent of the football pitch is empty. Ginger Bap stands alone on the wing. His hand is raised, and he's wagging his index finger. I think he wants the ball. He's waving his palms wildly. Now I don't know whether he wants the ball or not. *He* doesn't seem to know either. Finally, he shouts: "I'm over here." Nobody listens. Wishy has the ball and is running down the field with the butt stuck to his lips. He shoots and misses the net by ten yards. The other players cheer and jeer. Wishy shrugs his shoulders and goes for his Woodbine. Ginger Bap is agitated.

"Why didn't you pass it? I was all by myself."

"That's what I was afraid of," shouts Wishy.

"Fuck you anyway," rages Ginger.

Wishy withdraws his butt.

"Keep your head on your shoulders, will ye."

"This is cat, McGann. Shall we go?"

"Go where? What do you expect for nothin'?"

"Anywhere but here. This is rank."

I scan for some action. In the distance, I see a woman wheeling a big black pram towards the Tunnel area. She's either fat or pregnant. Probably both! The echo of a TV is suddenly audible from a nearby row of houses. A shadowy figure lurks at the Venetian blinds, peering through the slats. The other family members are probably planked on a big settee in the sitting room, paying attention to the box. Somewhere near the town centre, a motor is whirring. Likely a family of seven out for a Sunday drive. Window shopping day. The Town Clock interrupts proceedings with crisp unruffled chimes. Its intervention hypnotises me. How can something so loud and clear make me feel pensive and alone? The footballers seem to be playing in slow motion. Maybe I gave them too much credit a few moments ago. When the chimes stop, a deafening quietness descends. It's as if time has paused, and all that remains is existence. They play on silently—the ball talks, though not at all well. I live here in Portstown, a town as dead as a doughnut.

"Is that all the time it is," says McGann. I don't bother answering. I don't know the time. All I heard were the chimes. I heard them but didn't listen. There's a difference between hearing and *listening* to something; if McGann asks me again, that'll be my line of argument. He doesn't. We walk in silence. A frisson of fear races through me, from my big toe to my ears. What if all towns are the same as Portstown, with similar town clocks? When I get older, the only solution will be to go to a city like London. Big Ben must be different to this. It has to be, or I'm beaten.

We walk back up the hill. I hope that Lucy's still here. There she is, sitting on the seesaw opposite her friend. Her friend is no oil painting. She'd make a good match for McGann. Why is it that a good-lookin' girl always has an ugly one in tow? The contrast? You never see two good-lookin' girls together. It doesn't happen. One good lookin' one and a bag, that's the general rule. There's no such thing as a beautiful-lookin' girl being best friends with another good-lookin' girl. It's different for McGann and me. He's not *that* bad-lookin', and what he lacks in looks, he makes up for in personality. Plus, he's a boy. You don't have to be a good-looking boy to get a good-lookin' girl. But if you're an ugly-lookin' girl, the chances are that your boyfriend won't be an oil paintin' either. Snap! I wonder what it's like for an ugly pair. *You show me your spot, and I'll show you mine…mine's bigger than yours, so it is.*

"Slow down, will ye."
  I want to maximise the sight of Lucy. She's well–built with shapely fleshy legs. Her face is freckly but pretty with it. She's different to those girls that look like they've been suntanned through a tea strainer. There are gaps between *her* freckles. Her lovely brown eyes complement her soft complexion and her red hair. That revolting frizzy, marmalade, or ginger biscuit-coloured mop is not for Lucy. No…her hair is smooth and reddish, like a red setter's mane. It's loose, wavy and free. Clean and freshly brushed. No nits there, that's for sure. I can taste the aroma from here. It turns me on. I think I love her.

The next thing I know, McGann is walking towards the playground. No warning, no conversation. He has taken a left turn without any notice whatsoever. I'm still moving forward and screwing my neck sideways to see where he's headin'. Christ, he's going towards the see-saw. As if I didn't know! Now he's talkin' to the ugly one. He's got a fag in his mouth. He must be asking for a light. I hope he doesn't ask Lucy for a match because she'll probably say: "Yeah, your face and my ass." At least, that's what I hope she'd say. No, Lucy wouldn't be so blunt. Someone with beautiful brown eyes like hers couldn't be so vulgar. Look! He's friggin' well talkin' to her as well. He better not mention my name. She's staring at me now. It's one of those stares that happen when someone points you out. Christ!

I start pawing my face and avert my gaze. I think about posing, but I'm no good at that. My face is burning, and my legs are trembling. Adrenalin is swamping my stomach. I face forward again and continue slowly up the park hill. I hope to hell that he wasn't tapping her out for me. I hope he was. McGann's running towards me, trying to catch up. I don't slow down. "Hang your horses there, McCoubrey, will ye," he shouts. Only when we're safely over the brow of the hill do I turn round to acknowledge him.

"What were you up to back there? I hope you didn't mention me in your conversation?"
McGann gesticulates with his hands and puts on a sombre expression.
"I hope you didn't now?"
"I'm afraid I did, McCoubs."
Maybe he thinks that by shortening my name into its friendly and familiar form, I will forgive him, but he's got another thing coming if he thinks that.
"Tell me you're only kiddin'. What the hell did you say to her? Tell me now, will ye?"
"I told her you fancied her and that you'd sent me over to ask her out."
"You're a friggin' liar, so ye are."
"I'm not lying, McCoubs, honest to God, and I'm sorry to say that

she blew you out in bubbles."

A waft of heat surges through my face.

"You didn't really ask her out, McGann, did you?"

"No, *I* didn't ask her out, stupid. I tapped her out for *you,* and *s*he said: 'Not on your nelly', and then I asked her why not."

"And?"

"I don't think you want to know."

"I *do* want to know. What else did she say? Just tell me and get it over with, will ye."

"She said you were too small…. and if you'd have been a few inches taller, she might have thought about it."

"Are you serious?"

"Deadly serious….aye. I'm afraid she blew you out, McCoubrey… blew you out in bubbles."

"Jesus Christ, Jesus Christ… I'm showed up. I'm friggin' showed up…a few inches taller… I've never felt so small in my whole life. I could crawl under a snake's belly wearin' a top hat, so I could. It's alright for you, but I'm the one that has to face her at some stage. Why did you do it?"

"If she'd said 'Yes', you'd be huggin' me now, wouldn't ye, tell the truth now?"

"If my aunty had balls, she'd be my fuckin' uncle, wouldn't she?"

McGann doubles over with laughter.

"If the queen had balls, she'd be the fuckin' king," he splutters.

I wait until he's recovered his composure.

"Seriously, McGann, how am I goin' to face that Lucy one from now on?"

"You could always borrow your ma's high heels. I'm sure she wouldn't mind."

My head is in my hands, and I want the ground to swallow me up.

"What am I going to do…..you've just ruined my life, McGann?"

"Catch yourself on McCoubrey…have a titter o' wit for God's sake…. there are plenty of fish in the Bann."

"Aye, and they're all ugly pikes, so they are…yer girl Lucy's a bit special."

"Maybe she's not; she's a cracker."

"The only cracker I'll be getting' is a flippin' cream cracker. I couldn't get a kiss in a brothel, so I couldn't."

"You said it, McCoubs."

We walk home in silence. McGann breaks it.

"You could always marry a dwarf, ye know."

"Very funny."

"Seriously, it's a good way of savin' money. None of you would need to buy trousers. "

"What the heck are you on about now?"

"You could both wear turn-ups on your underwear....think of all the dough you'd save."

"I'm not that friggin' small, am I?"

I glance over, wishing to hell I hadn't encouraged him by mentioning the underpants joke about the dwarf from the football match. McGann shrugs his shoulders and stares pitifully at me.

"I'll see ye later, Charlie Drake."

"Cheers for that...thank Christ, I'm almost home."

Steel Comb

I can't believe my luck. There's a free seat in the kitchen. A miracle at last! I slump down, only to be greeted with shrieks of laughter from Lona and Ben.

"What's goin' on," I ask.

"You're sittin' in the gypsy chair, so you are," shouts Lona. "A gypsy woman was here beggin', and mammy let her in and even made her a cup of tea, and she sat there where you're sittin' now….haven't you smelled it yet … I can't believe that you can't smell anything, Barry-Joe?"

I jump up like I've got a scalded poker up my gravy ring. "Ahhhhhhhh…nooooooohh… you mean to tell me that a gypsy was sittin' in this chair, and now I'm sittin' there….why the hell did you not tell me before I sat down?"

"Because you didn't ask."

Ben and Lona are rolling on the floor, and my ma has a big grin stuck to her face.

"The poor woman wanted some food for her children… all I did was give her tea and sugar and a little bit of money for her daughter's First Holy Communion."

"What are ye on about?"

Lona chips in.

"Barry-Joe, she had her daughter with her in her First Holy Communion dress, and she was callin' at every house askin' for money. Even the Protestant ones! We peeped out the window and saw Mrs Pope slam the door in her face without even as much as sayin' hello."

 "And that's why I made a point of invitin' her in," says my ma. "I just wouldn't please those ones next door. Only I witnessed it with my own eyes, I probably wouldn't have let them come in, but I did it just for badness, and anyway, God says: Love thy neighbour, so he does."

"You mean the same way as you love the Popes next door?"

I like to inject a sarcastic comment now and again. It might be the lowest form of wit, but it's pretty satisfying if your timing's good.

"I'm not just talkin' about them, although with a surname like that, you'd think they'd be a bit more Christian, so ye would. It just shows ye that you should never read too much into a person's name."

"Unless we're talkin' about the Halfpennys across the road. Look at their name, and you can see why they're so stingy."

"That'll do, Ben," says my ma, but she's smiling.

"Not everyone is as generous as us. Yous might think that I'm a misery guts sometimes, but compared to some people, you don't know just how lucky yous are."

I'm standing in the middle of the kitchen, looking down at the chair in disgust.

"When I made my First Holy Communion two months ago, all I got was two pounds and twenty-five new pence," says Ben.

"You were lucky," I reply. "I got seven shillings and sixpence and a boiled egg for breakfast from the nuns."

"Aye, but that was years ago. Your seven and six was probably worth more than my two pounds and twenty-five new pence."

"It was only five years ago, ye know. I'm not that flippin' old."

My ma faces me.

"Don't forget about the Beatle suit I bought you for your First Communion from Littlewoods in Belfast."

"You mean the suit with no collar on it."

"That was all the rage then, so it was... I didn't hear you complainin' about it at the time."

"I didn't have much choice in the matter, did I?"

"You're the one that wanted it if I remember rightly."

"God, smell this bloomin' chair. Why don't you throw it out?"

"Why don't you give my head peace? I'll throw *you* out if you don't give over."

All of us are standing beside the cooker, staring at a wooden chair with a green plastic seat. I feel dirty. "Don't you dare touch me," cries Lona when I brush against her. Today is turning into the worst day of my life. First, I'm a midget, and now I'm a leper in my own house. My da is perched on the kitchen sofa, waiting for the news. He stares at me like he's waiting for my full attention. I pay it.

"Here, Barry-Joe, will ye go over to Ted Harbinson's house and swap papers."

I take our crumpled and stained Sunday Express and run round the corner. The pages are in the wrong order, and there's red sauce everywhere.

"My da says can we swap papers?"

Ted lifts the cushion of his chair and pulls out the Sunday Press, a Free State paper published in Dublin. Catholics buy it outside the chapel. Ted's reading a small newspaper that has an Irish name. I think it's called An Phoblacht. I know that "an" is the Irish word for *the*, but I haven't a clue what Phoblacht means.

"Cad é mar atá tú?" says Ted. I know that one. We learned it in O'Donnell's class. "Alright," I say. His face lights up. "Say that in Gaelic."

I don't know the exact pronunciation. "Tá mé go maith," he says... tá mé go maith...tá mé go maith. Tá mé go maith." So I repeat, doing my best to pronounce it exactly like him and succeeding. "I'll make an Irishman out of ye yet," he shouts gruffly as he gives me the Press. He checks to see what he's swapped it for. God knows why because it's always the same one. "Is that the best your da can do - the Sunday Express?" I observe him as he lifts his seat cushion and throws the newspaper underneath. "Bloody Sunday Express," he mutters and returns to the comfort of An Phoblacht.

The news is on back home. My da keeps shouting *Woust* at the slightest noise. My throat feels itchy, and when I feel a cough coming, I dart into the hallway, closing the door on my way out.

I retreat to the sitting room and cough in peace until I'm sure I won't be a burden when I return. The local news is starting, and that means Harry McCoubrey! He looks a bit serious tonight. His forehead is etched with wrinkles, and he's wearing a sober dark navy suit with a matching tie. No beige tonight! When he begins reading the news, my da says W*oust,* so I stop breathing and start listening.

"Serious rioting has broken out in Belfast today after a civil rights march. The fighting involved both nationalists and unionists. Twenty-six people have been injured; two are thought to be in a serious condition. The RUC have confirmed that twelve arrests took place."

Footage of the riots is shown. The police and a gang of civilians seem to be mounting a joint attack on a group of men, who respond with a flurry of bricks and bottles. One of the civilians is carrying a police shield for protection. How did he get that? I wonder if he borrowed it from a policeman or was willingly lent it. Some of their opponents are walking about, dazed and bloodied. They're shouting angrily as they pelt the police group with anything that can fly. These must be the nationalists that McCoubrey was referring to. "Get your ma for a minute, somebody," cries my da. We all shout "Mammy" simultaneously, and she arrives instantly.

"Rosemary, look! The police and the Protestants are attacking the Catholics in Belfast...they're in cahoots with one another."

"What's new?" replies my ma. "Jesus, those poor people haven't a chance, have they... where's it all goin' to end?"

I'm glued to the TV set, not wanting the action to finish.

Show me another few seconds of rioting. Let me see someone with blood pourin' down his face or a policeman passing a riot shield to a Protestant.

However, the footage does end, and the camera reverts to McCoubrey. He grimaces slightly.

"Now for the rest of the news. A twenty-year-old Protestant man has been stabbed in Portstown and is said to be in a critical condition in hospital."

"Woust," shouts my da. "Shut up a minute," cries my ma. I utter: "Shhhusss."

"It is believed that the victim was stabbed four times with a steel comb."

McCoubrey looks solemn.

"I wonder who it is," says my ma.

"It could be anybody," replies my da. "Whoever did it is either brave or a fool. Portstown's not the place to be goin' around stabbin' the other side. Somebody will pay dear for this, that's for sure."

"I wonder who it was," repeats my ma.

"Who, the fellow who was stabbed?" he replies

"No, the one who *did* the stabbin'."

"No doubt we'll discover soon enough, so we will."

"And that's this evening's news…I hope you've all had a pleasant weekend. I'll be back on your screens tomorrow at five thirty with the early evening news. I hope you can join me then."

A resigned expression covers his face. No parting joke tonight, though I can still see that McCoubrey twinkle in his eyes.

He's trying to tell us that better nights will come. Clearly, he's not comfortable playing the serious newscaster role. Leave that to Mr Bosanquet or Mr Baker. But why are you cringing, McCoubrey? Newscasters are supposed to be neutral and impassive, capable of delivering both good and bad news. Either way, it's only news. This little corny, pokey society isn't a bed of roses, McCoubrey. It's not all fun and games, ye know. Do you realise that? I think you do. You saw the riots with your own eyes. What do you think about the behaviour of the police? I know your answer McCoubrey… you don't have an opinion…you'd rather look the other way, read the sports news, and then tell a little yarn. Well, it's hard lines tonight, and no pun intended. Better luck next time. You can save your wee joke up for again. Rest assured; your day will come.

I go to bed wondering who's been stabbed with the steel comb. How the hell can you stab someone with a comb? I've got a steel comb in my pocket. It's better than the black plastic ones that catch all the dandruff, but it's blunt. When I comb my hair, I don't cut my skull or chop my ears off. I wonder if he combed his hair first. Or afterwards! Maybe he wiped the blood onto the sleeves of his coat, tidied his hair, and slipped the offending weapon into his back pocket. People who own steel combs are cool characters. I bet you he walked calmly from the scene. Only the black plastic brigade would scamper.

Both the stab victim and his assailant are from Brownsville. The guy in intensive care is known locally as Dinger Dodds, and the guy who stabbed him is a Catholic called Gerry Campbell. I know him to see. He has a tully eye, and it's hard to tell whether he's staring at you or himself. I never take any chances and always look at the ground on my way past him and for at least twenty yards after. I'm used to looking away from things and people. His nickname is "Soup" Campbell. Seemingly Dodds called Campbell a Fenian bastard, and Soup said: "I might be a Fenian alright, but I'm no bastard." Then he stabbed him. His comb had a hook on the end that had been sharpened. It was just like being stabbed with a knife. Now Dodds is rumoured to be on a life support machine.

My ma says that there'll be hell to pay if he dies. I ponder this. A dead man would be exciting, especially a dead Protestant man. That doesn't mean I'd approve of it. I've seen this guy Dinger about the place. He gives *everyone* dirty looks, especially young Catholic boys. Popey always says hello to him, but I keep my mouth shut. I think I'm ok because I hang around with Popey. But when I pass Dinger on my own, I can feel him leering at me, so I keep my head down and count the cracks in the pavement. Sometimes if I see him walking towards me, I start trotting as if I'm in a hurry to get home, but I'm merely trying to avoid his snattery gurning. He knows my religion, so I try to seem harmless when I go past him. I'm too young for any other approach, but I remind myself this won't always be so.

It has just dawned on me that *Dinger* carries a steel comb. He's one of these people who *stop* to comb their hair in the street. He loiters outside a local bicycle repair shop for hours, talking to those he likes and staring at the rest. The owner doesn't seem to mind. Perhaps he uses him as an unofficial bouncer if someone disputes the charge for fixing a puncture. I wonder if Dodds was stabbed with his *own* steel comb. I can't wait to tell my ma about my theory. Only a few people know this about Dodds and his comb. Not everyone is as perceptive as me. *There are no flies on you, McCoubrey, none whatsoever*. If Dinger does die, somebody will pay dearly. My ma's right about that one. Do I want that to happen? I'm unsure, as a dead Dinger would result in a dead Catholic or *two* dead Catholics. It would be a tit-for-tat situation. I'm probably too young to be the target of a hit, but it could be a relative of mine. It could be my da. Suddenly I'm shakin' like an orchard leaf.

The town is eerily quiet today. People mooch and huddle. I hear an auld doll saying: "People shouldn't be allowed to have steel combs unless they're a barber or something like that." I see the wheelchair man. He's busy gossiping to someone and doesn't acknowledge me. That's the last time I'll push him anywhere. When I pop into the Petrol Pump, the one-armed bandit watches my every move as I examine the goods. He's in the middle of a whispered tete-a-tete with some old boy and seems peeved that his conversation has been disturbed. Some people are relaxed about touching the merchandise, but I feel obliged to put my hands in my pockets whenever *One Arm* stares at me. Only when I have decided what I want to buy do I withdraw one of them, holding my bar of Caramac aloft, so there's no room for doubting my honesty.

"From next week, we'll only be accepting new money, no more old money like this," he says, taking my half-crown and throwing it carelessly into the till. He gives me my change in old money.

"And presumably, there'll be no more change like this," I say.

He glares. I continue:

"I mean, from next week, *everything* will be in new money, including the change."

I smile, but I'm not joking. It's my way of saying: *Frig you and your private conversations... I know fine rightly what you're talkin' about.* Suddenly I picture Dodd's coffin being lowered into the ground, and the thought doesn't bother me one bit. I don't give a fiddler's fuck.

I see Pope on the opposite side of the road and go over.

"Well, how's it goin'?"

He looks sheepish and pale and raises his chin skywards. "Ye know how it is," he says. "Ye know yourself." I want to tell him that I *don't* know! Otherwise, I wouldn't have bothered askin' him in the first place. But I bite my lip.

"Did you hear the news....about the stabbin'?" I'm trying to be friendly.

"Aye, it's cat."

"You know yer man, don't ye?"

"Aye, Dinger Dodds...it's cat boy. I'm not feelin' too happy about it, so I'm not."

"It's a bad business, alright, but what can we do?"

"I'd better run on here. I'm getting some messages for my ma. I'll see ye later, Barry."

"Alright, I'll see ye."

That's the first time he's called me Barry in years. I feel uneasy as I prefer Barry-Joe, McCoubrey, or McCoubs. Or even Kuri! "Barry" is too formal. Too strange! It felt like a goodbye just now. What's eatin' Popey? You'd think that somebody had stabbed *him* the way he was acting. I can feel myself gettin' annoyed and irritated. *He wasn't too friendly there, McCoubrey, not very friendly at all.* Dinger Dodds bounces up and down in my brain like the white keys on Tommy's piano. *No, not very friendly at all.*

In a town like Portstown, word of mouth travels faster than any telephone. Since most people don't have a phone, that's handy. If Dodds has died, we'd know by now. A woman in our street, Mrs Fraser, is a magnet for gossip. Any news worth hearing is filtered through Mrs Fraser's mouth. It's a substantial mouth, and when she's yapping, which is more or less constantly, she reminds me of the last gasps of a pike on the bank of the river Bann. She's a woman who never shuts her gob, and the day she does will be the day she dies. If Mrs Fraser hasn't heard it, it hasn't happened.

I observe her standing outside her house, on the footpath, waiting for the neighbours to approach her. She's so plump they'd struggle to walk past her if they wanted to. However, today they're pleased to stop for a gossip. Of course, they can only surmise, but for some, that's as good as the facts. As I walk around the cluster of women, Mrs Fraser performs a verbal somersault in mid-sentence:

"Hello, Barry-Joe."

She fixes her gaze on me until she thinks I'm out of earshot and might as well have said: "Cheerio Barry-Joe," because that's what she meant. So I walk on with my head bowed and in earwigging mode.

"A comb's for combin' your hair and nothing else...that's what I think anyway, and what's more.... "

"Try telling that to Soup Campbell," I mutter to myself. It looks like I'll have to wait on McCoubrey to get the latest.

"The victim of a sectarian stabbing in Portstown is said to be in a stable condition tonight, according to a hospital spokesman. The twenty-year-old man was stabbed with a steel comb while walking with a female friend on Sunday night. Police have arrested a nineteen-year-old Catholic man in connection with the incident."

McCoubrey looks relieved. He feels able to include his customary end-of-bulletin jibe:

"The Portstown soccer striker scored the winner in the preseason friendly against Glenavon. Unfortunately for him, it was an own goal, with Glenavon winning 1-0. Some you win, and some you lose," smiles McCoubrey.

I find myself sharing his relief at the stabbing news. But for how long? Dinger may have pulled through, but I think Gerry Campbell scored an own goal for the Catholics of Portstown.

"It's a good job he didn't die," says my ma.

"Why?"

"It just is."

"I bet you part of you wanted him to die. Tell the truth."

"Don't be stupid... why the hell would I think that?"

"You tell me."

"Tell you what?"

"You know what."

"I don't know... you're starting to get on my nerves."

"I heard that he was an Orange B."

"Wash your mouth out, will ye... if your da heard you comin' out with bad language like that, he'd kill ye."

"Well, I'm only repeatin' what I heard you say to my da... that Aunt Patricia lives in Brownsville near Dinger's house, and she told you that he was an Orange bastard who was always pickin' on the Catholics."

"Don't you be goin' round repeatin' that for God's sake Barry-Joe. She said he was a bad apple alright and that he'd probably been askin' for it. That poor Campbell fella's in trouble, and God only knows what his family are goin' to do now because they live in the same estate as the fella who was stabbed. They may get out of there as quickly as they can, so they may. We daren't open our mouths in this town... there are too many of *them* and not enough of *us*. This town is littered with bitter Protestants, and we're tolerated so long as we don't rock the boat. We're supposed to lie down and accept our lot. The Catholics of Northern Ireland are outnumbered. Most of them have poor jobs, but they survive. Poor houses, but it's a roof over their head. Too many children, but they can still eat bread and Champ. Accept the situation, and you'll get by in life. Catholics might be the poor relations of Portstown - the pennies compared to the penny halfpennies, but they can get by, which seems good enough for most of them. Very few people are prepared to open their mouths in this town. We daren't. As they say, a penny in your pocket is better than a slap up the backside. I'm not sayin' it's right. Of course, it's not. But that's the way it is, for now at least."

"Hmmm."

"So you'd better leave your steel comb at home from now on and use a plastic one instead."

"Why?"

"In case somebody sees you."

"Sees what?"

"Sees you combin' your hair."

"There's no law against combin' your hair, ye know. It's not a crime, is it?"

"Anyway, what do you need a comb for at your age…. are you a sissy or what? Will ye stop bein' an auld kittery, for God's sake."

"Everybody has a comb."

"You're not *everybody!* You don't have to be the same as everybody else. It's a plastic comb or nothin' from now on."

"In that case, it's nothin'."

"Suit yourself."

"Ok, I will."

"We'll see about that."

I lie awake for hours, thinking about Northern Ireland and Portstown. People are starting to kill each other in Derry and Belfast, and the ripple of death and danger is spiralling. I try to understand precisely why I hang around with Popey and play with other Protestant boys. I must like something about them, though it's hard to think what. I wonder what they see in me. Well, I'm friendly, like sport, and don't mind hangin' about the street providin' Crossroads isn't on. I'm one of the boys. But I'm also "handy", very convenient. I live next door to Popey, and we're the same age. Not too far to go to give McCoubrey a knock, and if he's not in, not too far to go back home. I'm nearly always obliging as I dislike hurting his feelings. It's a match of convenience. But, of course, there are differences. He's a boy scout and a TA cadet. His family are always the first in our street to fly the Union Jack - every year from late June. I'm the only Catholic he hangs out with, and he likes my family. Sometimes I feel that he thinks he's doin' me a favour. The token Catholic mate! He does acknowledge other Catholics when he's in my company, but it's a half-hearted hello or a simple nod of the head, and I think it's for *my* benefit. Maybe he thinks that I should be grateful that he's my buddy, but Popey doesn't realise that I'm not an appreciative kind of guy.

I notice his sly condescending looks when he passes other Catholic boys. *There are no flies on you, McCoubrey.* He probably thinks he's tolerating me most of the time, but I'm also tolerating *him.* This steel comb business has illuminated my thinking. I'm part of the Catholic flock. My future lies in the new Secondary School with the likes of McGann and Crozier or this new friend Murray. I know what side my bread's buttered, and I can tell the difference between Stork and real butter. You can taste real butter, but Stork melts to nothing in your mouth, like candyfloss. My friendships with Protestants are fickle and transient. They're going nowhere, slowly fading. I'll need to look elsewhere if I want something more lasting.

The rumour is spreading that Paisley is coming to town this evening. He's the guy that curses the Roman Catholic Church and ridicules the Pope. My ma once told me that Paisley kidnapped a young Catholic girl and held her captive for a week. She said that he went to gaol for this. He calls himself the Reverend Ian Paisley, a scary brute of a man - six and a half feet tall with size 16 shoes. I once read that his favourite meal is an Ulster fry. He probably cooks it on a pan the size of a bin lid. I must introduce him to Bonanza Bill!

At teatime, I notice a steady trickle of people heading out as I go home. I spot the Matchett twins, the Salvation Army boys. They're suited and booted like they're off to church. One of them looks like he's got big balls. What happened to the other twin? I'm dreaming about my tea, and everyone's streaming past me like I don't exist. They're headed for somewhere I'm forbidden to go. Tonight the town centre belongs to Paisley and his followers. I'll have to make do with eating Champ and watching Crossroads. I'm happy to go home, heading this way instead of the other.

His voice booms across Portstown. Redville's a mile away, but we can hear him. "Portstown is a Protestant town for a Protestant people." I can taste the menace in his voice. Digesting his words, I mutter: "Where am I goin' to live in that case?" In a caravan out in the sticks, beside the culchies? In a tent? Sorry for being born, Reverend Paisley. Incredibly sorry for being born a Catholic. Or, to give it its full title, a *Roman Catholic*. If *you* had been born a Catholic, would *you* be happy to live in a caravan in the middle of nowhere? No, you would not! I've heard stories about Catholics from Belfast fleeing to the Free State. Maybe Paisley wants us to do the same. I first visited the Free State a couple of years ago and was so impressed by its name that I brought hardly any pocket money. What was the point? When the shopkeeper charged me for a packet of Wine Gums, I was shocked. I remember fumbling for my change and hesitating, so he had plenty of time to change his mind. He didn't.

There's another more pressing reason why I couldn't live down South. All the teenage boys have yellow pimples on their pot-marked faces and dreary, sickly-looking skin. Although the girls aren't quite as pimply, most display either a mole or a wart at the side of their mouth. The warts look like erect nipples. It would be easy to tune into Radio Luxembourg! Their hair is plastered with grease and dandruff. They've obviously never heard of *Head and Shoulders* in the Free State. Watching a boy and girl walking down the street together is a sight for sore eyes - him with his pimples, her with freckly cheeks and big red warts.

The difference between Catholics and Prods in Northern Ireland might be between a penny and a penny halfpenny. However, the difference between a Northern and Free State Catholic is between having a penny in your pocket or being skint. The place is full of beggars. No, thank you, Reverend Paisley. I prefer to take my chance in Portstown rather than watch my two arms dangling the same length in Dundalk. These Free Staters are one rung above the gypsy who sat in our kitchen chair. The only thing free in the "Free State" is the air they breathe. And *it's* not the best.

The boom of his big mouth echoes into our house. My da turns the TV up and shouts "Woust". He's talking to us, but I know it's aimed at Paisley. McCoubrey comes into view on television, and my da says: "That man's got a big mouth." He's not referring to the person on the screen. My ma closes all the downstairs windows, but we can still hear the drones of the big man. Ben chips in:
"I wish he'd shut his big mouth and give his ass a chance."
"Don't you be rude," chides my ma, laughing her head off.
My da turns the volume up defiantly. The drones are mostly drowned out, and we take comfort from watching the box.

Black Balls

Brendan Batten calls unannounced with a towel under his arm. The school sniffing episode is history.

"Do you want to go to the pool," he says.

"You could have given me a bit of warnin'."

"I'm givin' you some now."

"Wait a minute."

I scurry around the house looking for a clean towel and end up with a thin, worn-out one that looks more like a dishcloth. Stuffing my trunks inside the towel, I look for a plastic bag. There's no way I'm carrying this item under my arm. Batten also has a plastic bag, but it's full of empty Domestos and lemonade bottles. When we get to the Petrol Pump, Batten goes in to change his empties into money. I wait outside. There's no way I'm going in there to be shown up. Peering through a gap in the window, I watch *One Arm* slap the empty bottles onto the counter. He then passes some change into Batten's hand and turns to serve a real customer.

"Did *One Arm* give you your change in new money, Batten?"

"Aye, I made sure he did. I was watchin' him like a hawk."

Batten's a good swimmer. He does lengths, and I do breadths. We meet up every few minutes and exchange a few words.

"It's lovely and warm, isn't it," he says.

"What, the weather?"

"No, the water, you eejit... what d'ye think I'm talkin' about?"

"How many lengths have you done?"

"I haven't been countin'."

"I think it's about five or six."

"I think it's six."

He knows *exactly* how many lengths he's swum and how many he will swim. I like disturbing his flow because it makes me feel better about doing only breadths. He swims away, and I wonder if he'll piss in the pool. If he does, I hope he does it in the deep end. Four more breadths, and I'll have done ten. That'll do me. Thinking about Batten has made *me* want to go. I must drag myself out of the water and walk a few yards to the male toilets. Mind you, he's right about one thing: It *is* lovely and warm here.

After we've showered, we go to the changing cubicles. The row is full of noisy children, shoutin' and roarin'. Someone starts to sing: "We all live in a yellow submarine," and everyone joins in. WE ALL LIVE IN A YELLOW SUBMARINE, A YELLOW SUBMARINE, A YELLOW SUBMARINE. Again and again, they chant the chorus. Some Smart Alec knows the first line: "In the town where I was born lived a man who sailed to sea." We all join in: "Dededededede…dededeeee…dededeee….WE ALL LIVE IN A YELLOW SUBMARINE" ….

I'm into the song, but I hope this guy with all the words doesn't milk it. Christ, there he goes again. "IN THE TOWN…." Someone shouts: "Shut your gob and give your ass a chance." "Fuck you," he replies. The changing rooms fall silent. Everyone's glad they're in the sanctuary of a cubicle. I finish dressing. *I* didn't tell him to shut up, so he needn't come bangin' on my door. "Are you almost ready there, boy?" I say, tapping on Batten's cubicle. "Aye," he answers and appears looking fresh and clean. We walk down the hushed corridor, and Batten stops at the electric hair dryer. "Have ye any change for the dryer," he says. "You're the man with all the change," I reply.

"Shall we call into Jack Mortimer's for a laugh?"
"If you want," says Batten.
Jack's shop hasn't been cleaned for years. The big glass sweet jars are covered in dust.
"Have you any Brandy Balls, Jack," I say.
"What?"
He's deaf.
"Have you any Brandy Balls?"
"Yeah, Brandy Balls, yeah."

"Can I have a quarter of Midget Gems instead?"

"No Brandy Balls? Midget Gems instead?"

"That's right Jack… Midget Gems instead."

He takes them slowly from the jar, one by one, until the scales approach 4 ounces.

"Anything else?"

"No, that's all Jack."

I pay him, and Batten starts to edge out of the shop.

"Hang on a minute there, Batten….Jack, have you any Black Balls?"

"What?"

"Black balls."

"Black balls?" He looks at the various jars.

"I've got some Black Balls," he shouts.

I've already started to snigger and desperately try to prevent it from becoming an unstoppable laugh. Of course, McGann's better at this than me, but I've started, so I might as well finish.

"In that case, why don't you friggin' wash them?"

Jack looks puzzled, but when he sees us laughing, he shouts something about the police. I squeeze past Batten and scarper down the road in fits, feeling full of myself. When Batten catches up, he's smiling but not laughing, like me.

"He said he's goin' to call the cops."

"He doesn't even have a phone, for God's sake."

"Have you done that before?"

"No, but McGann and Crozier do it all the time. Here have a few of these Midget Gems. I've been eatin' them non-stop since some girl said I was too small for her to go out with me."

"Very funny! Are you serious, McCoubrey?"

"Unfortunately, yes… that frigger McGann went behind my back and asked her out for me in the park last Sunday."

"Who is she… do I know her?"

"You probably know her to see, but I'd prefer to keep it under my hat."

"You don't have a hat."

"I know I don't, but I'd still prefer to keep it there anyway."

Some guy's car has stalled, and he's standing at the driver's seat, looking around for a few suckers to help him push it. I look around as well, but it's too late. We've just crossed into a side street, so there's nowhere to hide. Of course, we could always turn back, but we might bump into Jack and the cops. He smiles as we approach. Bingo!

"Hi ye lads, you wouldn't give us a wee push, would ye… the motor's stalled on me, so it is? Have yous been to the swimmin' pool?"

I can see him staring at Batten's skimpy towel. Finally, we rest our gear on the back bonnet and lean into the bumper.

"After three," he says. "One, two, three," and we start pushing like billio. He's walking at the front, steering the wheel. Then he gets into the car and closes the door. He starts to watch us out of his front and side mirrors. I mutter to Batten: "The lazy frigger's only steerin' and expectin' us to do all the work." He's pantin', and I'm pantin'. Twice the man tries to start the engine, but it splutters and then dies. "One more try, lads," he shouts. "Keep 'er goin'…give her lalty." We try desperately. "Come on," we both shout in unison. The car engine builds momentum, and we shout: "Now come on, ye girl ye." "*Now*, hit it," I roar. It doesn't matter that I don't know what he's supposed to hit. The engine starts to rev, and then it roars. He doots the horn at us as we tramp back to the footpath. Soon he's on his way, still gaping into his mirror as we pant for breath and I fumble for the Midget Gems.

"It would have been nice if he'd offered us a lift."

"Fat chance," says Batten. Did you not see the Orange sash in the back seat?"

"What are ye on about?"

 "I saw it through the back windscreen when we were pushin' the thing."

"Now he tells me….if I had known he was an Orangeman, I

wouldn't have bothered my ass. He must think that we're right mugs. Do you reckon that he knew we were Fenians?"

"Wise up. Of course, he knew. Did you not see the smirk on his face when the jalopy started movin'?"

"No, I didn't, but if I'd known that he was a Jaffa, I wouldn't have given him a push in the first place....I'll tell ye that for nothin'."

I have to get a few messages for my ma in Hetty's. Batten goes to the sweet shop next door. The fruit and veg shop is quiet. There's only one other customer who's still making his mind up. Then, just as I reach the counter, he opens his mouth.

"Do you have an Iceberg?"

"What's that dear?"

"It's a lettuce."

"I thought you meant iceberg like in the Titanic. Ahh, an Iceberg lettuce! I've got you now. I'm not thinkin' straight today at all. Sorry, dear, we've none left. They all seem to have melted away." She starts laughing at her wit, and he starts grinning. Her eyes are looking into his, and she creates a fresh laugh. He starts to laugh at her, then pauses. "All melted away... that's a good'un alright, so it is." More hearty laughter ensues. I'm bowled over (my ass) by her sense of humour and remember my mother's wee piece of advice about sarcasm being the lowest form of wit.

You're a real comedian, Mrs. Comedienne, I should say. Remember your ma's words, Barry-Joe. Remember now!

I look at my Swiss watch. Hint! Hint! They don't take any notice. So I cough. She notices *that.* "I hope *he's* not looking for an Iceberg as well," she shouts to her customer, nodding in my direction. Then they *both* start laughing. I acknowledge them with the most artificial smile and move towards the counter.

"Could I just have a bunch of bananas, please...whenever you're ready?"

On my way out, I notice a slanted cardboard box full of oranges on display. An image of a battered Ford Cortina enters my head. The driver is wearing a bowler hat with a bright Orange sash draped proudly over his shoulder. He is smirking. In his rear-view mirror, he sees two stranded young fellas. One has something under his arm, and the other boy is bent double, holding his knees. Both are staring at the Cortina. The driver winds the window down and waves vigorously with his right arm. His smirk becomes a grin.

Two flippin' mugs, that's what we are!

Batten's waiting for me at the doorway, towel under his left arm, a comic in his right.

"What did you buy?" I ask.

"The Beano."

I walk on as if nothing has happened. I'm praying that he doesn't start reading it in the street. Buying a comic like that is bad enough, but at least have the decency to hide it inside your towel until you get home. I might bump into somebody I know around here. If he starts reading that thing, he'll likely begin to laugh out loud, and then he'll want to show me what he's laughing at. So I'll have to try to laugh even though I don't get it.

They do it at school all the time...passing the comic to the guy behind, people running over desks to join in - usually over *my* desk and *my* elbows. They all huddle, and when one of them giggles, it's like a row of bloody dominoes falling everywhere. I feel like a leper, but I'd rather be a friggin' leper than read the BEANO or the DANDY. It's not simply because I don't get the joke half the time. No, *I don't want* to get the damn joke. Comics bore me to death, and so do people who read them. Batten's no pansy, but if he opens that thing near me, he can go to the swimmin' pool by himself next time round.

The Tartan Gang

No sooner am I through the door than Lona shouts: "The Tartan Gang is comin', the Tartan Gang is comin'." I glance at my ma.
"What's she on about?"
"You'll never believe it."
  "Believe what?"
 "You'll never believe it, so you won't."
 "What's goin' on...are you goin' to tell me or not?"
She looks pale, and I can tell that it's something important.
"We've been threatened... all the Catholic families have been warned that they've three hours to get out of their houses or they'll be burnt out."
"Burnt out by who?"
"By the Tartan Gang."
"Who told you that?"
"Some fella from Obins Avenue came knocking on all the Catholic doors to warn us. He accidentally knocked on Mrs Allen's house, and she told him she was a Protestant and an Orange woman. He told her she needn't worry in that case, but I've just noticed that she's gone and hung up her Union Jack for all the world to see."

Mrs Allen is a posh woman who lost a leg in a car accident a few years ago. Since then, she's been driving one of those bubble cars that disabled people use when they can't drive normal ones. They only have three wheels and look like something you'd get for a Christmas present.
"All she cares about is her own skin," says my ma. "If she was a Catholic like us, she wouldn't have a leg to stand on."
"Sure, she doesn't have a leg to stand on already."
She laughs.
"The same one can get by better with one leg than I can with two. Never mind that. Your da's not home yet, and I've no way of

tellin' him until he arrives. I wish to hell he'd hurry up because I don't know what way to turn. I don't bloody know whether I'm comin' or goin'. How are we supposed to defend ourselves against that lot?"

She looks solemnly at me, Lona and little Ben.

"You may all start prayin' to God… and I'm not jokin' either."

Although my nerves are jangling, I retain an image of one-legged Mrs Allen. Maybe the stylish solitary high heel on our coal shed roof is hers. Unfortunately, it's too fancy for my ma!

We are standing at the sitting room window. Everything seems normal. Most of the other neighbours take it in turn to pull their curtains and look outside. We stare at them, and they stare back. Then, finally, I spot my Aunt Lizzie. Her house doesn't have any curtains. She stands at the darkened window like a statue. I'm beginning to think she *is* a statue because she looks motionless. There's no way I'm budging until I'm sure she's real. She keeps me waiting until she finally lights a cigarette and sits on a chair at one of the alcoves of her window, her face pressed close to the glass. It looks like she's settling in for the duration.

When my da arrives from work, the house falls silent. We're waiting for my ma to tell him the news, but she serves his dinner as usual. He's eating in the kitchen, and the rest of us are toing and froing from the sitting room, waiting for her announcement. I'm bursting to tell him, but something warns me that this luxury should belong to my ma.

"Have you told him yet?" I mutter.

"Not yet," she replies. "Let him eat his dinner in peace."

The rattle of his fork fills the kitchen. I'm facing his hunched back, keeping my distance. He's been out since seven o'clock this morning. Twelve hours spent working on a building site. Christ, I couldn't. No way! My mother's right. Let him munch his food in peace. I'll copy my aunt Lizzie and make myself a nice cup of Rosie Lee. I see my ma at the sink, doing the dishes.

"Do you want a cup of tea?" I ask.

"I could murder a nice cup of tea," she replies.

He stares blankly at her when she tells him the news and takes another slurp from his cup. Then he asks her to go over it again so that he fully understands the background.
"I blame that kern Paisley...comin' down here and windin' the people up and then bailin' out when his dirty work has been done. You heard him with your own ears. '*This is a Protestant town for a Protestant people.*' When his own side hears that type of thing, is it any wonder they decide to go on the rampage?" He bites a chunk from his Paris bun and continues talking with a full mouth.
"I wonder what Ted Harbinson thinks of it all. I can't see *him* takin' too kindly to anybody tellin' him to get out of his own house."

We proceed to the sitting room. At the bottom of the street, a lone figure stands in the middle of the road, Hurley bat in hand. He's wearing a long raincoat even though it's one of the best nights of the year. It's Mr McCall, a quiet schoolteacher with a harelip. Now and then, he prods the ground with his stick as if he's checking its sturdiness. His chest is out. Any invaders will have to get past him first. McCall's an unlikely hero, sort of private and serious. He still lives with his ma even though he's over thirty and gets narky if a football lands in his garden. Soon a few more Catholic neighbours crawl out of the woodwork and drift towards him. Now we've got the makings of a street defence force. I'm old enough to get involved in this. On the way out behind my da, I tell my ma to keep everyone away from the windows. I might as well talk to the wall. She's gazing at us as we approach the ragged group outside McCalls.

The atmosphere is subdued. A few nods and quiet hellos are exchanged. Someone says that he was enjoying his dinner and watching Crossroads and that he hopes the Tartan Gang don't take long, as there's another programme he wants to watch later on. My da is leaning against someone's car, smoking and listening, while one of our neighbours speaks seriously with him. I can tell that they're worried. Some children have gathered boxes of bottles and stacked them under the bumper of McCall's car. An upstairs window opens, and Johnny Creally pokes his head out before producing a shotgun. He's laughing. Someone grabs his hair and drags him back inside the room, closing the window with a bang. I feel both scared and elated. I'm afraid because I know that this is for real. Delighted because I know that Johnny Creally's older brother would use that shotgun if he had to. I've seen him out hunting in the fields, rifle slung over his shoulder, preying for rabbits or pheasants, anything that moves. And if anything *does* move within view, he's quick on the draw. He hates to miss, and on the rare occasions this happens, we young ones know that it's best to fade out, to make ourselves scarce. Even though he kills animals, Creally's brother prefers *them* to people. *I* know that, but the Tartans don't.

I catch my da's gaze, and he gives me a knowing look. There's no attempt to chase me home. This time I have a role to play. I'm accepted. Suddenly a car swings around the corner and stops behind us. Two guys in bomber jackets get out and approach. They babble to my uncle Ted and some older men, including my da. Then they drive off as suddenly as they arrived. I notice a look of disappointment on the face of some of the men. My father is smiling wryly. It usually means that he's feeling either cynical or disgusted.

We hear the sound of a Lambeg Drum. It grows more threatening as it comes closer. Then it stops. A weird, muffled silence ensues before the first cluster of denim-clad youths is visible. Some have covered their faces in red tartan scarves. Others don't care and walk forward casually as if they own the street. The stream of people continues until a gang at least one hundred strong is thronged at the bend of the road, just a few yards from our house. I pray that my ma has closed the Venetian blinds and that Ben and Lona are safe from the windows. *Why did we all gather outside McCall's house anyway? There are several Catholic homes before his, for goodness sake. Are we expecting the Tartan Gang to simply ignore them? What's goin' on?*

The chants begin:
"Fenians out, Fenians out…Fenian bastards out."
There are mostly men, with a smattering of women and children in their ranks.
"Fuck the Pope and the Virgin Mary."
They've edged forward and are now precisely outside our house. I look at my da.
"They're outside our bloody house."
No reply.
"Jesus, what are we goin' to do?"
No one answers. McCall flexes his arm and swipes his Hurley bat through the air. A few of the older boys tighten their belts. One of them strokes his chin endlessly. Malachy Madden buttons his duffle coat, and the man my da was talking to blows his nose. Glass clinks as bottles are emptied from a large cardboard box. One by one, people lift some. "This is it," shouts someone, seeing that the snarling Tartan Gang is barely twenty yards away. "This is it boys."
They move towards us in slow motion. Some of them are quiet, others mouthing obscenities. I can see the hatred in their bulging eyes. Crystal clear!
"Fenian bastards, dirty Fenian bastards. You were told to leave, but yous wouldn't listen, ye Fenian scum."
The ringleaders are tall boys wearing buttoned Wrangler jackets. They're walking towards us. I'm hidden behind our group, waiting for the charge to begin. I spot a boy I know from football, Ivan Rowntree. He's at the back of the mob, wearing his royal blue Rangers top. Ivan is a wimp on the football field, so I'm amazed. If I were him, I'd get offside.

No charge! Instead, a volley of bottles and stones rain down upon us. We see them travelling through the air and turn away. Malachy Madden uses his duffle coat as protection. Instantaneously we reply. I throw my bottle extra hard in case I decapitate one of us. A few of them scatter when they hear the sound of broken glass, but the rest keep coming, trotting but still not running. Whoosh! McCall's Hurley bat thuds into someone's jaw, and I jump backwards in shock. I see a Wrangler jacket with a person inside it, writhing on the ground. Bottles and bricks rain down. At least six of us are hit, including my da. Blood is trickling from the side of his head. It's a free for all, hand-to-hand, fist-to-fist.

The road is narrow, so they can't easily surround us. Only about thirty are game, driven on by bitterness and pure hatred. The majority hang back, yelling and threatening. They fire stones through a few windows and retreat. I feel a terrible thud on the back of my head and turn to face a wild animal. "Fenian fucker, you little Fenian cunt." His fists are raised as if he's waiting for my reaction. Time stands still…then I thrust towards him at speed. Fist and boot at the same time, and again and again. The few early successful hits charge my adrenaline, and I kick him into someone's garden. Then I become vicious, treating him like someone here to kill me.

I pause for breath and realise I'm standing in McCall's rose garden. I've no energy left, so I step back onto the street behind the unabated mass brawl. The road is littered with bodies, and blood stains are visible on the black tarmac. I search out my da. He's grabbing a teenager by the hair and kneeing him in the face. I want to help, but I'm knackered. Most of the Tartan Gang are mere spectators. A few suddenly run and land a few digs before trying to retreat. Some succeed. Others don't. I see a bottle being smashed on someone's head. Is it one of our heads or one of theirs? *How is this goin' to end*? I look for inspiration at Creally's window and see it. A rifle barrel appears, and an almighty cracking sound rips through the street. I duck and cover my head and heart. Another thunderous crack! I shut my eyes and pray we'll come out of this alive. I can hear a dull commotion around me. Peering through my fingertips, I watch the Tartan Gang scattering. The guy I left in McCall's garden escapes behind us. We see him hobbling, and someone fires a stone that misses, but no one tries to catch him.

I notice some of them charging through our front garden without stopping and feel elated. Luckily we don't have any roses! Soon our group are unopposed in the street. McCall emerges with a bloody mouth and retrieves his Hurley stick from the side of the road. He's panting and smiling and mutters something, causing blood to seep from his mouth. Wiping the blood on the sleeve of his overcoat, he exchanges a few more words with the older men. Then, as he ambles up his driveway, he examines his rose bed. He shakes his head and wipes his mouth once more.

We sit in the kitchen drinking tea. I'm given a full cup for once. Suddenly I realise I'm in the gypsy chair and notice it doesn't bother me. "IRA," says my da. "Indian Reservation Army is more like it, all right."
"What are ye on about?" says my ma.
"The people in the car were IRA men, but they scampered at the first sign of trouble. Irish Republican Army, my ass. I Ran Away is more like it."
He bites a big chunk from his Paris bun as if to say: "Who needs them anyway?" My mother pats his forehead with a damp cloth as he lies back in the armchair.
"Sit still for a minute, will ye, Danny."
Ben and Lona stare in his direction but don't talk. I dip my Marie biscuit into my tea.
"What if they come back tomorrow night," I say. "What's goin' to happen then?"
"Now you're talkin'," says my ma. "They won't be too enamoured that we've defended the area… they probably didn't expect that and probably thought they could walk all over us."

I tell them I saw Pope in the middle of the Tartan gang, and Lona cries.

"Yes, Barry-Joe ...I peeped out the window at one stage and saw him with a brick or a bottle in his hand ...one of the two. He was right in the middle of them all, so he was."

My ma is flustered.

"I don't want you hangin' about with that git anymore, Barry-Joe. He's a bad egg, so he is. I'm sorely tempted to go and knock on his bloody door this minute and give him a piece of my mind. He must have known that our family was one of the ones that were threatened by the Tartan Gang."

"Don't bother your ass," shouts my da. "Hopefully, he'll have learnt his lesson tonight."

"I wouldn't put money on it," she replies.

No Paper Today

Snippets from last night's drama replay in my head as I cycle through Redville on my way to the newsagents. Neither the sun nor the neighbours are awake. I enjoy my paper round, especially as it's the school holidays. When I reach the shop, the owner Mr McGurty helps me to fold the newspapers into a cardboard box. The headlines in the Irish News bang against my head: *Portstown Man Dead After Petrol Bomb Attack.* It's the Conway family from number 82 Ridgeway Drive. I glance at McGurty and realise he already knows. If he thinks I'm goin' to deliver a paper to a dead man's house, he's got another thing coming. No chance!

"See what you think when you get there," he says. "It mightn't be as bad as you think...the police will probably be there."

We fill the box in silence. McGurty doesn't understand that I'm *already* outside the house of the dead Catholic guy, and I won't touch that letter box with a barge pole. Not a hope in hell!

As I cycle from the shop, there's only one thing on my mind. *A dead Catholic in Portstown!* I'll reread the story after my paper round. There's a spare copy in the box, marked number 82. *Doesn't McGurty realise that dead men can't flippin' read? Does he really expect me to put a paper through their letter box so the family can read about what happened to their son and brother only a few hours ago? Business is business, eh? I can't understand it!*

My heart pounds as I approach Ridgeway Drive. I still have to deliver a paper to number 88, three doors away. I see a solitary policeman on the footpath outside Conway's house. The street is dark and eerily silent.

Did the neighbours go to sleep as usual after they heard the bang? Maybe some of them had their regular nightcap of Ovaltine and toast. Or they used the occasion as an excuse to have a bonus. Two Ovaltines for the man in number 78. Hot Chocolate and toast for the couple in 84 next door. Why do Irish streets progress in twos, with even numbers on one side of the road and odd numbers on the other? Why not consecutive numbers, just for the paper boy?

The yellow paper blinds are down in every room of Conway's house. Black scorch marks plaster the downstairs front window and walls. I desperately try to park my bike silently outside number 88. Tip-toeing to the door, I slide the paper inside the letter box. My heart is thumping, and it almost explodes when I feel someone grab the newspaper from inside and hear the clack of the letter box as it slams shut. Shuddering with fear, I flee down the pathway, leaving the garden gate ajar as I escape the ghost of number 88. Head bowed, and with bated breath, I walk my bicycle past Conway's scorched house, and round the corner, before hopping on. Breathing heavily, I cycle away, steadily at first, then furiously. I whizz through my Brownsville deliveries like a man possessed. I'm escaping from death, every furious pedal ushering me to safety. Momentarily, I wonder what is happening inside Conway's house. Is anyone at home, or are they all at the hospital? I'll never deliver a newspaper to this estate again. Better still, I'll never deliver another newspaper to *anybody's house* after today. It won't matter whether they're dead or alive.

The Conways used to live in Redville. They were neighbours of Mrs Fraser, according to my ma.
"What do you mean you can't remember them ...they all had ginger hair...all the sons and even the daughter was a redhead? I can't believe that you don't remember them. You remember them fine rightly, so you do. They all had buck teeth as well, like the McBrides."
Once she provides the teeth detail, she looks eagerly at me. I've got no choice but to remember the Conways, with their ginger hair and buck teeth.
"I can sort of remember them now. Did they *all* have buck teeth?"
"Oh, for God's sake, you're getting on my nerves, so you are. You

even used to play with one of them, so you did…when you were a child."

"Was that the one with ginger hair and buck teeth?"

"They all had…I'm warning you now…I'm not in the mood for any of your stupid games, ye know."

"I do remember him. Eamon was his name."

"That's him, Eamon…..the both of you used to catch the bus to school in the morning, but he's not the one who was killed. It was the eldest one who died. Charlie, you called him, and he was only seventeen years old poor *crater*. It makes you realise what could've happened to us the other day, so it does. You may all say your prayers because things are starting to get bad in this place, and God only knows where it's all goin' to end."

She looks drawn and serious. I can tell she's worried, so I make her a strong cup of tea - not too much milk, two sugars and stirred anti-clockwise for good luck. She fetches a currant square from a crumpled white paper bag hidden under the cushion of the gypsy chair and slumps down to enjoy a well-deserved snack. We all watch, willing her to relax and enjoy the moment.

Vice Versa

I head to the hop at the Variety Hall. However, I can't see much variety here - girls with gurning faces, an ugly one in tandem with a plain looking one, wherever you look. They *own* the small cramped dance floor. The fellas are allowed to saunter around the perimeter but can only trespass into the middle if a girl agrees to dance with any of them. Crozier and I walk around two or three times, each journey similar to the last. Finally, we retreat to a side balcony area to observe the action. They're playing a **10cc** song called "**Rubber Bullets**".

Load up, load up, load up, ruuuuberbullets, load up, load up, load up, ruuuuberbullets.

The confident lads start asking the girls to dance, and the floor is soon packed. I watch them dancing, observing the girls giggling at some whispered words in their ears.

"Screw your man feeling yer girl's ass," shouts Crozier. "He's elected. Maybe he's not."

I stare intently at the ass. "Maybe he's not," I reply. "Maybe he's not."

We stroll around the hall.

"What about those two in the corner?" he says. "You take the one on the right, and I'll take the other one."

I gaze over. The one on the left is pretty enough, but mine's Fatty Arbuckle.

"Wise up, Crozier. Do you think I came up the Bann in a bubble? There's not a cat's chance in hell of me askin' that one to dance. She's a fat boot, so she is."

"She's not that bad, is she? Alright, c'mon then, and we'll have another walk round."

I traipse behind him until he halts next to another two girls. "Would you like to dance?" "No thanks," she says. Then he tries her mate: "Would *you* like to dance?" "No thanks," she replies. We're in Indian file, and Crozier repeats the exercise three times. Different girls. Same response! He perseveres, but the next "victim" doesn't bother replying. So he shouts louder in case she hasn't heard him the first time, and this time she ushers her friend onto the dance floor, leaving the two of us standing there like lepers. "Frig this," says Crozier. "Follow me, McCoubrey." I obey. Soon he stops beside another two.

"Would any of yous two girls like to dance?"

They start giggling, and then one says: "Alright." She goes to get up, and I hear Crozier say: "Don't bother your Barney because I wouldn't." He walks on, and I freeze, not knowing whether to laugh or cry. The girl is speechless and sits back in her chair as if she's been hit by one of *10 cc's* rubber bullets. She's no oil paintin', but I feel sorry for her, even though I'm stifling severe laughter. I shrug my shoulders, feigning puzzlement at Crozier's behaviour. "I'll dance with ye sure," I shout. She looks at her friend, and then *I* look at her friend. Permission is granted, and we manoeuvre into the thick of things. It's a slow song halfway through, so I hurriedly get into the smooch position.

I CAN'T LIVE
 IF LIVING IS WITHOUT YOU,
  I CAN'T LIVE,
I CAN'T GIVE ANYMORE,
I CAN'T LIVE.

The song captures me, forcing a meek surrender to its words. She's not *that* ugly, and with a bit of imagination and a few more sung words, she seems pretty. The song fades, and reality arrives. Will she stay on the dance floor or walk away? Part of me wants her to walk, but I don't want to get shot down either, especially by a plain one. She doesn't budge, and we stay for the next song. It's too fast so it doesn't suit me! I don't know how to dance, so I prefer smoochy songs. When it's over, we mumble something inaudible to each other. I think I caught the word "toothpaste". I'm glad she didn't hear me because I don't imagine she knows who won the 2.30 at Haydock Park. We shuffle away from each other, she to her girlfriend and me to the safety of the side balcony.

Mitch is on the dance floor, jiving with a girl. He's a good jiver, and I'm jealous of how he can twist his long gangly legs and bend them to the beat without the right one bumping into the left. I can spell rhythm. Crozier *has* it. I manage a smile because I know Crozier isn't too bothered about girls. He prefers the *gee-gees.* I want him to succeed as I watch him whisper sweet nothings in her ear. She bursts out laughing. Not a smile or a smirk. No, that was a proper laugh. The frigger has impressed her, and she's not that bad looking either. She's one of those girls who doesn't need to stop dancing to hear what the bloke says. She continues to swing and twirl. Spinning round from another jive, I catch her grinning at Mitch, big front teeth like the McBrides, only sexier. Christ, it looks like he's elected, the lucky brat.

He joins me on the balcony, full of himself.
"I'm in there, McCoubrey…how did you get on with ugly chops?"
"Cheers… she's not that bad lookin', is she?"
"Is the Pope a Catholic?"
"Thanks for that, Crozier…I don't give a shit. Go and tap her out for me, will ye?"
"If you say so. I'm meeting mine at the park gates in fifteen minutes, sunshine. There's a hole in the wire, so we can get in no problem."
"When you tap her out for me, don't be acting the bollocks, do you hear me?"

Me and Crozier are standing at the park gates. I'm trembling from head to toe, but he's not. They arrive together, and we clamber through the hole in the wire. Mine catches her cardigan, but she doesn't complain. We walk in twos, me and Mitch ten yards ahead.

"Let's head over to the benches beside the cricket pavilion," he says. "It's nice and dark over there...they won't see what's goin' on."

We both look around to check that they're still in tow. I can hear them giggling. That's all these girls seem to do - giggle. I hope they're not laughing at me, so I do. Mitch planks himself on one bench, and I do the same on the other. She sits down beside me on my left. I'm tongue-tied. She's beside the other girl on Crozier's right, and they're twittering to each other. I glance over both their shoulders at Crozier. Within seconds he is leaning over his girl, dolling her like billio. I hear them shuffling and notice his hands clasping around her neck. I can't decide whether he's being intimate or about to strangle her. He's onto his second kiss, and I'm still talking about school. She looks bored, and she knows that I know she's bored. I don't know how to stop diggin' this hole. My palms are sweating, and my face is flushed.

"So why did you ask me out anyway?" she whispers expectantly. I feel the sentence: *It's nothing to do with looks if that's what you're thinking,* flash through my head, but I manage to stifle it. I open my mouth to give some reply, and she leans forward and covers it with her big lips, circling them furiously while pressing into mine. I'm suffocating, but her breath is hot and steamy, so I copy her circles. Round and round we go. It feels nice, but I'd like to live until I grow up. Eventually, she extracts her mouth from mine, and I pant like a dog. "You're not a bad kisser," she mumbles into my ear and lunges at me again.

This time I'm ready for her. I push the back of her neck forward until we're locked together, and I can feel a large piece of flesh exploring the roof of my mouth. When she releases, I consider saying something sarcastic to tell her it was *tongue-in-cheek*. There's no point. She won't get it. *Don't bother your ass,*

McCoubrey. Instead, I draw her close and stick my tongue beside hers. She licks. I lick. She licks at an angle. I do the same. She mustn't like this tit-for-tat because she suddenly reverts to *lips only.* Now I can relax, as I sort of understand this technique. I just need to make sure that I remember to breathe.

"You're getting better at this, aren't ye?"

"Vice versa."

"What do you mean vice versa…are you insinuatin' that I'm a bad kisser?"

"Not at all."

"Well, I expect a bit more than vice versa, you cheeky imp."

I can feel the bumpiness of her bra strap through the back of her jumper. She doesn't flinch. My heart races, and I manoeuvre to her front. The heaviness at the side of her chest guides me, and I slide my hand fully into position.

Something smashes into smithereens near my feet. Milk bottles! Startled, I jump up from the bench. I hear laughter from the back of the cricket pavilion and rush to confront my attackers. They're already clambering out of the hole in the wire, and I soon recognise the voice of Boot McConville.

"Is that friggin' you, Boot? Come 'ere I want ye a minute."

A shadowy figure turns round. It's him, all right.

"No, McCoubrey, it's not me; it's *Bare Ass,* you eejit," he roars as he disappears into the night with his accomplices. My blood is twisting with frustration. The moment has passed, and she's standing beside the bench, ready for the road. We head back towards the Variety Hall in silence. Crozier remains draped around his piece of stuff, totally unfazed by the sound of broken glass.

Back in the Variety Hall, she says: "I'll see ya around," and returns to her mates. I catch her grinning as she approaches them. This makes me feel good. You don't grin if you're not happy, do ye? She must have *something* to smile about. Her mate gawks over at me, and *she* grins. This is getting better by the minute. I stand there like a statue, pretending I haven't noticed any of this, but I've seen every sneaky glance and scrap of body language. Now both of them are dancing in a small circle. My girl's ass is swaying gently. Nothing outrageous or deliberate. Just a subtle movement! Although I don't think she's flaunting it, I'm delighted there's no hiding place for my disco dancer's backside. *Wherever you go, miss, it's goin' to follow. Yesssssss....giddy-up there ye girl ye.....giddy-up. Maybe I'll have another crack at her sometime. Why not McCoubrey? Why not, indeed?*

The Collection

An uneasy calm has covered our street since the Tartan Gang rampage a few days ago. The parish priest calls. He greets my mother outside our house. She's at the bread van.

   "Is anybody dead, Rosemary?" he says.
"Why do you say that, Father?"
"Because you're wearing black."
It's not a prompt about Conway from Brownsville. Just sheer nosiness! If I pulled the dog collar from his neck, what colour would he call that? My ma could ask him the same question he's just asked.
"I'm just wearing black for a change," she replies meekly.
She means that she's got nothing else to wear that's clean. In the house, she serves him tea and fresh buns she bought from the bread man. His timing is good today. When he called a few months ago, she took a considerable risk. "Would you like another few biscuits, or are you full up," she'd said. She had emphasised the *full-up* bit. Thank God he took the hint because we had no more biscuits to give him. Each time he comes, she offers him tea, and his reply is common to all of Portstown's priests: *I'm only after one.* He means he's just had a cup in number 24, but I always think: *One's all you're gettin', Father.* I'm happy to twist the meaning of things to satisfy my quirks. There are no exceptions for Nosey Parker priests dressed in black.

He slurps from our best Delft and scrutinises his Paris bun before each chunky bite. I'm observing *him,* wondering if he will talk to it or eat the damn thing.
"You've got a nice set of teeth when you smile, Mrs McCoubrey.
"If you don't mind me asking, are they false or real?"
If I were her, I'd take them out right now and try to say "Cabbage"

with a mouth full of gums. That would answer his question. But, instead, she says: "They're the only teeth I've got, Father. That's all I can tell you." It's a good answer. He smiles and takes another mouthful of his bun.

Father Brady is still in the house when Mrs Fraser knocks.
"Isn't it terrible?" she splutters.
"Isn't what terrible?" replies my ma.
"Poor Janet Jeffries has been shot dead by one of her own. Seemingly she was footerin' around with a gun belongin' to her fancy man, and it went off. It blew half her head off, they reckon. And she was such a good-lookin' girl and all. The whole thing's hard to take in. I can't believe it myself."
"I bet she's not too pretty a picture now," I mutter. My mother is tut-tutting, and the priest looks pale and concerned. A chunk of the bun is glued to his mouth, and he can't decide whether to eat or withdraw it. Eventually, he pushes it in and gulps some tea. "That's shocking news indeed," he says, setting his cup on the fireplace. "Shocking news indeed, very upsetting." He looks on the verge of tears but composes himself with another slurp. "You see Mrs McCoubrey and Mrs Fraser...in a town like Portstown, this is a very worrying development, as I'm sure you both appreciate."
I appreciate it too, but it seems that I've been excluded from this part of the conversation. It's for adults and priests only.
"Where in the name of God does that leave us all," he asks.
"You tell me," says Mrs Fraser, "for I don't know."
"I don't know either," replies my mother. "But one thing I *do* know is that there'll be hell to pay."
"God help us all," the priest sighs as he fumbles for one last Rich Tea biscuit.

Jeffries' death consumes me. For such a friendly girl, she's obviously fond of keeping bad company. I correct myself-*was* fond because now she's "brown bread" (*cockney slang for "dead" that I have recently learned and an expression that tickles my fancy*).

She'll never smile again nor stride past our window in her blue Ulster Laces uniform that couldn't disguise her slim, attractive figure. Had I been a few years older, I'd have tapped her out. She'd probably have blown me out in bubbles, but it would have been worth the embarrassment.

What was going on beneath her cheerful exterior? She was only a teenager, but I bet she knew about sex. I wonder if the guy gave her one before she blew her brains out. Maybe she went out with a bang in more ways than one. Who was that bullet meant for? Some innocent Catholic from Portstown, that's for sure! I imagine Jeffries playing her little game of Russian roulette with the gun's owner. She deserved to lose, so she did.

After tea time, there's a knock at the front door. It's Mrs Fraser and another woman. Mrs Fraser takes charge.

"We're collecting for poor Janet," she says. "She was only seventeen, and her family are in total shock, God love them. They can't believe what's happened."

I'm standing behind my ma in the hall, waiting to see if she'll go through with what she said earlier. She doesn't disappoint.

"If she'd died any other way, I'd be the first one to put my hand in my purse, but I can't bring myself to give money for someone who was playing with guns. Why was there a bloomin' gun in that house in the first place? That's what concerns me. What was it for? I suppose it will all come out in the wash. Anyhow, I'm very sorry, but I'm goin' to have to say "No" as far as this collection is concerned. I've nothin' against the girl, and I feel awful for her family, but I just don't feel right about givin' money under these circumstances, and I hope you can understand where I'm comin' from."

Mrs Fraser turns purple and is speechless. The other woman hasn't opened her gob and mournfully turns to leave. My mother gently closes the door, and through the small glass pane, I see the bulky frame of Mrs Fraser waddling down our garden path. We all peer through the sitting room window and watch them until they turn the corner. Out of sight and out of mind. My ma looks pale.

"You did the right thing," I say. "You were one hundred per cent right to do what you did. So don't feel guilty about it. Why should ye?"

She sits down.

"I think I need a cup of tea," she sighs.

I jump up.

"I'm goin' to make you one because you deserve it, so you do… you did the right thing there, and don't think that you didn't."

The man from Hewitt and Gill's calls, and it's a relief when he's allowed through the door. What a bonus! He's unaware of what happened beforehand and settles into the settee, his green tweed jacket still buttoned. He licks his fingers and expertly flicks through his notebook until he finds our records.

"There we are, Mrs McCoubrey…it comes to fifty new pence."

She gives him a green pound note, and he digs a shiny coin from his pocket.

"Fifty new pence for me and the same for you….this new decimal currency takes a bit of getting used to."

I'm staring at his brown bristly moustache: *Yeah, about five minutes was how long it took you to get used to it, Mr Hewitt and Gill.* I reckon that his gravelly voice could sell oilcloth all day long. If I offered him my pocket money, I wonder if he'd continue talking for a bit longer. I wonder how many sentences I could get for twenty new pence?

I think I'll stay in tonight. *Take Your Pick* has just started, and the silky tones of Michael Mile's voice waft through the kitchen. My da has just heard the news from Lona about Mrs Fraser's collection and brings another cup of tea for my ma, with the last half of Paris bun. So we sit glued to the screen, waiting for someone to win the booby prize. "Take the money or open the box," shouts Michael Miles in a voice as smooth as his name. I imagine a conversation between him and the man from Hewitt and Gill's. I'm observing it, a cup of tea in one hand and a Paris bun in the other.

It's your turn to say something. Not too much at once now. Give the other person a chance, will ye? Ok, you can talk now.

Laughter erupts from the screen.

"He's won the booby prize, Barry-Joe," shouts Lona: "A pair of women's tights."

Giddyupthere

I'm studying the runners and riders for the Derby, which is on TV. The first thing I do is look for a particular jockey. Lester Piggott! If there's a major flat race, Piggott will be riding in it. It's a strange name...Lester Piggott. His first and surname are weird, and when I see that he's riding in the Derby, I stop and stare. The name of the horse he's due to ride is secondary. It's *Piggott's* horse! In close-up shots, he usually has a scowl on his face. The more I see him, the more I think Lester looks like a horse. Sometimes it feels as if he *is* the horse.

The horses and jockeys are down at the start, circling. One of the runners has spread a plate and is being attended by a blacksmith. Some horses are sweating. From the corner of my eye, I see a shot of Piggott. He has dismounted and is standing under a tree holding the reins, keeping his mount cool. The tree is a reasonable distance from the starting stalls. It's as if he's trying to hide the animal; for both jockey and horse to become invisible. My best mate from primary school Mitch Crozier, is a big Lester fan. He's always mimicking him. Sometimes Mitch whips his bum cheeks with his right hand for encouragement.
"Go on, Lester. Giddyup there, boy, giddyup."
I'm sure that Crozier has backed Piggott today. It's a big race, and he always has a bet on these. I'll cheer Lester on for us both.

They're under starters orders, and they're off. Piggott immediately goes to the front of the pack. He's trying to dictate things. My da is in the kitchen with me, watching the race on our small black and white TV. When I glance at him, he doesn't give anything away, even though he has a betting docket in his hand. A few horses challenge Piggott's for the lead, but he always seems to be just in front. On the wide outside, one looks like it has overtaken him. However, Piggott's on the inside scraping the paint from the rails, and when the camera angle changes, he's still in front by half a length. I'm feeling very nervous now because they're into the final straight, and I can see a few challengers making headway, just behind the leaders. Piggott's bottom is in the air, glued to the rest of his body. Both parts are eerily still. I check my da. His mouth is open, and it doesn't suit him. He moves forward in his seat. "Go on, Piggott...let him go," he roars at the telly and then shouts: "Woust," just in case I'm about to talk. He needn't worry, as the drama ensures I'm afraid to breathe!

Piggott whips his horse thrice in quick succession as if by magic. Whack, whack, whack! It starts to scoot clear, galloping like billio towards the line. My da has lurched forward, half standing, half sitting. He taps on his thigh in a steady rhythm, just like Crozier.

"Go on, Piggott. Bring home the bacon. You're the man. Go on, giddy-up, ye boya".

I check if anything with hooves is pursuing Lester, but the other horses are toiling in his wake. Also rans! As he goes past the winning line miles in front, Piggott shows no emotion. In the close-up TV shot, he is stone-faced. I'm picturing my da and Crozier collecting their winnings and calculating my percentages. It's looking good! Da sinks back into his armchair, clutching his betting slip.

"Piggott's some jockey boy," he declares, without looking away from the box.

Short Back And Sides

It's haircut day. I gape into the window, and all the barbers stare back without stopping work. They seem to say if you're coming in, come in, and if you're not, then don't. I enter and sit in silence on a spare wooden chair. A man sits beside me, and a child gets "Short Back and Sides". The man is taking a keen interest in proceedings. He must be the child's da. When he engages with the barber, I study him. His dark mop is getting straggly, so I wonder if he's next ahead of me in the queue. He stands up when the barber applies Brylcreem to the boy's head and pays him shiny new money, saying: "That's dead on Victor."

I'm beckoned to a red leather chair, and a thin white cloth is stuffed down the front and back of my neck. The barber swivels the chair until I'm in his preferred position. He cuts the air with his scissors.

"Short back and sides?"

"Yeah, and can you take a bit of the top as well?"

"I can do whatever you want, son. Just say the word."

He's chopping away, twice on my head, three times in the air. Occasionally, he digs his hand into my jaw and jolts my head from side to side. I'm watching intently in the mirror as the operation progresses, and I don't like what I see. Finally, he goes to his shelf and picks up a pair of hand clippers. He clicks up and down my neck. Ouch! He's just nipped me. And again! "Short back and sides never hurt anyone," he barks as he shoves my head down. *Not until now!* My chin is on my heart, and I'm trying to redirect my eyes upwards to see what's happening. If I can sneak a look in the mirror, I'll be able to keep an eye on Sweeney Todd, and hopefully, he won't wholly butcher me.

I locate the wall mirror and snatch the reflection of a denim-clad youth behind me.

"Have ye any of the other Victor?"

"And what other might that be?"

"Ye know yourself, Victor…have you any Frenchies?"

The barber allows me breathing time while he hokes in a drawer under the sink. Then, he hands a small packet to the youth in return for some change.

"Don't be doin' anything that I wouldn't do," chuckles Victor, but the guy has gone. "He's a flippin' eejit, that fella," he says, slapping Brylcreem into my skull and shaping my hair with a steel comb. Then, finally, he permits me to examine the back of my head for two seconds and frees the cloths from my shirt collar. I give him thirty new pence and tell him to keep the change. It's lucky I did since none has been offered.

I check my new haircut in the window of the shop next door. *That's cat McCoubrey, friggin' cat. There's no way you can buy broken biscuits lookin' like that.* My plan has been scuppered, and I trot home so no passers-by can dwell on my short back and sides. I speed up when I see the Wheelchair Man. If he only sees the back of my head, he won't be able to recognise me. There's no way I'm pushing him with short back and sides. He can wait a couple of months until my hair grows back.

Butlins Here We Come

I'm off to Butlins tomorrow with Mitch Crozier and Mickey Murray. I've only got to know Murray recently, even though we've been in the same class for six years. He's just moved to Redville from the countryside and seems to have adapted well to an environment without cows and pigs. His ma and da go to Butlins every year and have agreed to take Mitch and me, provided we pay towards our chalet. Mitch will pay my share, as he's kept his winnings from the Derby. Good old Lester Piggott!

"I've bought you a new shirt for travelling in," says my ma. "So hurry up and try it on before I iron it will ye."
It's three sizes too big.
"Look at the size of it… what size is the collar? 15! Sure, my da takes a size 15."
"You'll soon grow into it."
"Aye, when I'm about twenty-five."
"You haven't tucked it in properly."
"How come it's touchin' my knees then?"
"It'll do fine rightly. Do you want it or not, because if you don't, I don't fancy traipsing the whole way back down that town to change it. They mightn't even change it anyway because I bought it in the sale."
"How much was it?"
"Too friggin' much…anyway, it's not that warm…you can wear it under a coat."
"You mean hide it."
"Give it to me. You're wearing it whether you like it or not."
"I'm only goin' to Butlins. Does it matter what I wear for the journey?"
"You could be goin' to Timbuktu for all I care …but you're not showin' me up in front of people, so you're not."
"In that case, I'm going to be sittin' in Murray's car with my coat

buttoned."

"And you can button your lip while you're at it…and after you've had your tea, you may have a bath. I'm not havin' Murray's mammy talking about us, so I'm not. She was *Black* before she was married, and her sister Nora went to school with me."

"Was she *Black* as well?"

"I'm talking about her maiden name. Murray's ma was called *Black* before she got married."

"Oh, I see what you mean now."

"You'll leave my house spick and span, and after that, it's out of my hands."

"Can't I just wear my Slappy Joe instead of the shirt, for the car journey?"

"I'll pretend I didn't hear that remark. I've never heard such a rigmarole over a bloomin' shirt…there you are…it's ironed and all for ye. Hang it up in the wardrobe."

Oh, we're all off to Dublin in the Green, in the Green, With the Helmets Glistening in the Sun.

Murray's ma is in great heart. She turns to the three of us in the back.

"You fellas don't mind if I sing a wee song on the way down?"

"No, Mrs Murray, go ahead and sing away."

I'm trying to be sociable.

"If we said that we minded would it make any difference?" says the da.

"No, Jimmy, it wouldn't."

She cackles with laughter, and we all join in.

Oh, We're All Off To Dublin…………

I'm wearing my Slappy Joe. We slow down at the Irish border, but the Gardai wave us through.

"It must be dinner time," says Annie.

"Are you referring to them or to us, Mrs?" says Mr Murray.

"Both."

"In that case, we'll stop off in Dundalk for a bite to eat."

The mood in the back seat relaxes further.

"That's the best thing you've said all day, ma," shouts Mickey.

"Have whatever you want, boys," says Jimmy. We all order fish suppers, and Mickey asks for beans with his. Mitch looks at me, and we both look at Murray. He's sitting back in his seat, rubbing his palms together.

"You'll enjoy Butlins boys," says Mrs Murray. "We go every year, and it's great. We were going to go somewhere different for a change this year, but it's hard to break old habits, so it is. Isn't that right, Jimmy?"

"That's right, Mrs."

She's blowing rings of smoke into the air.

"Could you not have waited until after your dinner until you did that?"

Mrs Murray doesn't reply. Instead, she looks at us and tilts her head towards Jimmy.

"You see what I've to put up with every day, boys. But, sure, a wee bit of smoke never killed anybody. Isn't that right, Barry-Joe?"

"That's right."

This is great. Fish *and* chips, for the second time in my life. The first time was when I received my First Holy Communion money and had to pay for it myself. And for my ma's! It had been my idea.

"You didn't have to do that with your precious money," she'd said as we left Malocco's. "But I must say that I enjoyed it, so I did… it's a pity you couldn't make your First Holy Communion every week son…the more's the pity."

We pass each other the salt and vinegar bottles by sliding them along the Formica table. Apart from that, we don't converse. Finally, I feel the need to say something.

"These chips are good."

Silence! No one is paying me the slightest bit of attention. My intervention has been useless, and I desperately wish I'd just concentrated on my grub, like Mitch and Murray. The latter burps unapologetically, and his ma smiles. We all look at him and laugh. Thank God I'm off the hook for once.

A guy a few tables away has a wart on his forehead and greasy black hair. He has pimples on his red nose, and one of them is big and green. Both he and his girlfriend are smoking. They are lingering over a mug of tea. I can't see much in the way of conversation. It looks like the morning after the night before. Her dark mini-skirt hugs her big fat thighs, and her shabby black cardigan is holed at the elbow. She has scrab marks on her face. He cracks a little joke, and I notice that she's got nice smiley teeth and a sad friendly face. They're not bad people. Just skint! Not a rap between them. I'd like to pay for their tea, but that would depend on Mr Murray paying for *my* fish and chips. What happens if I pay for the two teas and Murray's da doesn't deliver? I'd be up the swanee in a canoe without a paddle. Moreover, I don't want to squander my holiday money on the first day, do I? *Don't worry, McCoubrey, it's the thought that counts, and you're too young to insult adults by offering them twenty new pence.* I settle back in my seat, satisfied by my dinner and particularly pleased that I devoured it before I spotted the neighbours.

Our car is parked beside a shopping parade. I notice an ice cream van nearby. *Mr Whippy*! My mother has given me a shiny fifty new pence coin to buy sweets or ice cream for the trip as a thank you to the Murrays. I've considered trousering it, but Murray's da has paid the dinner bill for everyone, meaning my spending is intact. The allure of Mr Whippy erases the tinge of sadness I'm still feeling about the café couple. As requested, I order two pokes for the adults and three 99s for the boys. Clamping the five cones into my cupped hands, I shuffle back to the car in robotic baby steps. My concentration levels reach an intensity that bomb disposal experts could only die for. As the cones are extracted one by one from my rigid palms, I can gradually breathe. It's a great relief to be sitting contentedly in the leather back seat of the Morris Minor with my *99* for company. *Murray's da bought the fish and chips, but I got the ice creams. Mission accomplished!*

At first, I smell it. Then it rises and drifts around the car like it owns the place. Poisonous! I look at Mitch, and he nods towards Murray. Someone's about to get the blame, but it better not be me. Only one of us had beans, and it wasn't me, so it wasn't.

"What blurt farted? Christ, that's terror altogether...that's friggin' cat, so it is."

He winds the driver's window the whole way down. Mrs Murray lights another fag.

"Jesus, boys, that's serious...could yous not have waited until we got to Butlins?"

"It wasn't me," says Mitch. "It must have been one of these two."

Mrs Murray looks at Mickey and me.

"Well, whichever one of yous did it, it's bloody stinkin'." She rolls her window down.

"Stinkin's not the right word for it, Mrs...it's friggin' atrocious, so it is. Terror altogether!"

His face is red.

"Was that you, Mickey?" he shouts.

"Nope."

"Are you sure?"

"Yip."

She looks behind from the passenger seat, laughing. "Somebody let off and didn't let on boys." Then, as her laugh becomes a loud guffaw, I catch him looking in the mirror...at *me.* He's shaking his head and tut-tutting, so I feel compelled to defend myself.

"It wasn't me. Honestly, it definitely wasn't."

Mitch is on my left, and Murray is on my right. They both point simultaneously at me.

"McCoubrey let off and didn't let on," cries Mitch.

"That's cat McCoubrey," says Murray. "Could you not at least have held it in until we get there?"

Bye-bye, Pimpletown. Hello, Butlins holiday camp. As we swing into the car park, I notice nothing special. The place is packed, though; it takes five minutes to find a space ample enough for Murray's da to park his Morris Minor. We head to our chalets. Me, Mitch and Murray will share while Murray's folks are in the next row. The other two boys quickly claim the top bunk beds, and I've my pick of the bottom ones. I choose the one under Mitch since he didn't have beans either. Then I carefully hang up the shirt that's too big for me, alongside a bright pair of blue trousers - my Sunday best - and a checked sports jacket that's also too big. I can't decide whether I'd rather have a large shirt or an oversized coat, and I lie on the bed, flustered about it. Murray farts.

"What are ye doin' down there, McCoubs...are you scratching your ass or what?"

Shirt or jacket, jacket or shirt? I'm contemplating this, but I realise he has shortened my name. He's only known me properly for about six months, and I've gone from McCoubrey to McCoubs. What is it with these people?

"Probably the jacket."

"What are you friggin' on about McCoubs? I didn't come the whole way from Portstown to sit in a wooden cabin listening to you gibberin', so I didn't. So what do ye say, Mitch?"

Mitch farts. "That's all I've got to say."

"Ok ...if it's goin' to be friggin' competition between the two of ye, let's go then."

They both hop down and off we head.

"Screw yer man."

We look over at a guy on the putting green. He's wearing a Panama hat and Tartan shorts, and his belly is flopping over his crotch. The putter is in one hand, and a large sugary doughnut is in the other. He doesn't know whether to take a bite or have a putt. He pushes the doughnut into his mouth and chips with his free hands. When he removes the doughnut, three-quarters has disappeared.

"Look, he almost got a hole in one," shrieks Mitch.

"No, he didn't," I retort. "The ball's nowhere near the hole."

"I'm talking about the *doughnut,* you simpleton."

"Oh, I see what you mean now."

"Big fat Free State slob," mutters Mitch.

"Is that all yous can do?" says Murray. "Slag other people?"

"Why, can you think of anything better to do?"

Mitch is smirking.

"Aye, I'm going to get some of them friggin' gravy ring doughnuts. Just lookin' at that hallion has made me hungry."

The scent from the doughnut stall grabs me by the short and curlies. I want to eat *it* and *then* eat the doughnuts. We watch them sizzle and turn golden. I don't know whether I will work around the crispy circular edges or bite straight into the middle. Two aul dolls are ahead of us in the queue. They've ordered two each, but when these are ready, they order another two. I knew it. Now I'm goin' to have to starve for another two minutes.

"This is cat."

I'm addressing Mitch and Murray.

"This is friggin' cat."

"Would you flippin' hurry up, Mrs," mutters Mitch, "because I'm about to faint with hunger."

"Anybody would think that yous two hadn't had a bite to eat all day," says Murray. "I'm still pretty full after my dinner…I think I can only manage three myself."

"God help him," says Mitch, nodding at me. "He can only manage three of them."

We dander off, scoffing our hot doughnuts. Heaven on earth! I've one in each hand and one in my mouth. I use the back of my right wrist to bury the one I'm eating. I mustn't be too slow, or one of those two will try and pinch one. Mitch was there on the day of the Hot Chocolate. Where food or drink is concerned, you couldn't trust him as far as you could throw him. To be doubly sure, I slow down and walk five paces behind the other two. This is better. I've got them covered. I quickly stuff the other two into my gob, hurting my throat as I swallow. When they look around,

I'm licking my sugary fingers. Job done!

"Would you screw that? It's a swimming pool made of glass."
It's Mitch.
"No way."
"I'm telling ye…come 'ere til you see."
Mitch is pointing upwards, and sure enough, I can see a boy in goggles, swimming underwater.
"Screw yer man under the water," shouts Mitch. "With his goggles and his flippers. Who does he flippin' think he is - Jacques Costeau?"
Murray stares at the guy.
"He thinks he's *it,* so he does, the little Free State git."
"How do you know he's a Free Stater?" shouts Mitch.
"Any chance of me getting' a word in edgeways?"
I'm spluttering, fearful that I'll miss my moment. So I dive in.
"Because he's got big juicy pimples all over his nose, so he has."
"He's wearing goggles, so how can ye tell?"
"I just can."
"They're a big pair of goggles and all."
"You're getting' on my wick Crozier."
"Aye, he does that sometimes," laughs Murray.

I still can't get to grips with the pool. What happens if the glass breaks? If I throw a stone this second, I could watch one hundred people swimming on concrete. Christ, it's temptin'. Maybe it's not glass. It could be Perspex. Stronger than glass! Harder to break with stones! I'm desperate to find out what it's made of.
"Shall we go for a swim, boys?"
"What, straight after the doughnuts? "Let's wait til tomorrow mornin'… c'mon and we'll head over to the amusements."
Since his da gave us the lift, we feel obliged to follow his suggestion. "I bet you they're not all they're cracked up to be," says Mitch.

I spot a miniature train. "Look, boys….a model train. Let's have a go on this before the amusements." The train has open carriages big enough for six people to squeeze in. It's full of Butlins revellers having a holiday within a holiday. It travels on a track shaped like Figure 8, and there are a few model stations along the route where people can get on and off. We go to the guy at the entrance gate and flash our Butlins' passes. "The next excursion will be in five minutes," he says, talking like a proper station clerk. "Form an orderly queue now. You can disembark at any stop along the route, but you need to decide in advance whether you will do the full trip or part of the trip and let me know so that you get the right coloured ticket."

"This is some palaver boys. Where do yous want to go?"

"The whole hog," says Murray. "I'm knackered anyway."

Mitch approaches the man at the gate.

"Can I have three return tickets, please?"

"Where to?"

"To here."

He says it with a solemn face.

"All the return journeys start and end here. I said you can get off at another stop along the way if you want."

He doesn't realise that Mitch is taking the mickey. Either that, or he's not one little bit amused. Perhaps he's had a sense of humour bypass, like all the ticket collectors in Ireland. Mitch should realise that middle-aged baldy men don't laugh. It's not in their nature. They stare, gape, huff and puff, look perplexed, and occasionally manage a glimmer of a smile, but a good laugh is off the radar. They work as Ticketing Clerks, Lollipop men, Policemen, and Car Park Attendants. All they need is a uniform and a little bit of power. Sometimes they're in charge of the toy trains at Butlins.

"All aboard for the Butlin's Express."

"Express? I thought he said that we could get off," says Mitch.

"It's only a figure of speech," replies Murray. "Leave the old boy alone...he's only doin' his job."

We've got a little carriage all to ourselves. The sun is out, and I lie back and dust a few crumbs off my Slappy Joe. Now I can concentrate on my trip. The toy train chugs along at about five miles per hour.

"There's no roof on this yoke," shouts Mitch.

"What do you expect for nothin'?" says Murray.

"Agghh, sure, you can't beat this boys."

Mitch gives me a dirty look.

"Can't beat what?" "Sure, the friggin' jalopy's hardly movin'. I could walk faster than this."

"Except you don't want to bother your poor little ass Crozier, isn't that right?" says Murray.

"You've got it in one."

I sit up.

"You've given me a good idea there, Mitch."

No reply.

I hop off and run alongside. All the Butliners are gaping at me, and I can feel their stares. The train seems to go faster than I thought, swerving around a bend just as I'm about to lurch back on.

"Giddy-up there, Jesse James, that'll teach ye," scoffs Mitch.

"Come on, Arkle. You'll have to do better than that."

They lie back like lords as the toy train diverts to the right, leaving me stranded in no man's land.

"See ye back at the ranch Jesse."

"Go home and play with your Scalextric like a good boy."

"You should've bought a return like us."

"You were too big for your boots, McCoubrey."

"You lost McCoubs. You lost."

"Adios, amigo!"

Teatime is between five and six pm for today's arrivals. The queues start to form at four-thirty. I spot the gravy ring doughnut ladies right at the front. One of them is eating a packet of crisps. Eventually, we are ushered to our table. The hall reminds me of our school canteen, but we don't have to share a table with other guests. I don't like eating beside people that I don't know. Although, come to think of it, I'm not too fond of eating beside people I *do* know. Having Murray's parents here is bad enough, but total strangers would be ten times worse.

Sausages, chips and beans! We dig in. I munch slowly until I see Mr and Mrs Murray engrossed in their food. We soon finish a whole loaf of sliced bread, and Mrs Murray has to ask the waitress for another one. "They're growing, fellas," she laughs, and the waitress smiles back. "No problem at all," she replies. "Just give me a wee minute." I'm not sure what the difference is between a *wee* minute and a *big* minute, but when she returns with a pan loaf sixty seconds later, I'm not bothered any more.
"Well, what did yous get up to this afternoon?" says Murray's ma. "Have yous tried the gravy rings yet?"
We reply in unison.
"Aye."
"Good God, I could murder one of them this minute, so I could."
I've no doubt in her case, she means a wee minute.

I notice a respectable-looking family staring at us from a few tables away. You'd think they'd never seen a hungry person before, the way they're gawking. I pat the napkin on my mouth, hoping that this will give me an air of respectability. Unfortunately, it doesn't work because Crozier knocks his plate off the table while I'm wiping crumbs from my face, bending over to pour his fifth glass of water. Total silence envelops our section of the restaurant, and I expect big oohs and ahs as they do in our school canteen when this happens. However, the silence endures, and I hear the steely clicks of the knives and forks from the respectable table. It's business as usual over there. Mitch takes a redner and gets down on his hunkers to retrieve the broken Delft. I look at Murray's ma. She's lighting a cigarette. "Don't fret, son. Sure it's only a plate, for God's sake. It would have been worse if there'd been anything on it."
We all laugh, and normality resumes.

We're off to the bumpin' cars, and I'm nervous because I'm not much of a driver. I tried this lark once before in Portstown and got hemmed into the corner of the track while all the other cars took turns to ram me. So, once bitten, twice shy, I hook up as a passenger with Mitch. But, Christ, he's not much better than me, so he's not! We both laugh when we get rammed the first few times, but after that, it gets real.

"Frig this for a game of cards," cries Mitch as he tries to manoeuvre backwards, only to get slammed again. I look around and see Mickey laughing, steering wheel in his hands.

"That was Murray."

"Who does he think he is…Stirling fucking Moss?" "I'll get him back in one wee minute. So hang on to your hollyhocks McCoubs."

"Christ!" He tries to go forward this time, and the car takes off. We're moving freely but in small circles. I feel like I'm in the middle of a clock. Then, bang! We jolt forward, and Mitch bangs his head on the steering wheel. "Who the fuck was that?" he screams. We both look around and there they are, big grins across their faces. It's Pinky and Perky, the two jolly doughnut ladies.

"I can't believe those two pigs have bumped into me," screams Mitch. "Who do they fuckin' think they are?"

Five minutes later, our suffering is over, and I vow never to ride in a bumpin' car again. On the way back to our cabin, we meet Murray's parents. Mrs Murray has plastered her hair with lacquer, and Mr Murray sports white trousers, a checked green shirt, and sandals.

"We're just going for a wee drink. Once I get my Babycham and some country music, I'll be dandy. We'll see you all at breakfast tomorrow."

She addresses Mickey, but it's meant for the three of us.

"Behave yourselves now, won't you?"

"Are we in for the night?" says Mitch as he clambers onto the top bunk.

"Aye," says Murray.

"Aye," I sigh. "It looks like it, but I wouldn't mind one of those gravy rings."

"Me too," says Mitch.

"Is that all you two hungry hallions can think of?" roars Murray.

"Yip."

After stuffing ourselves at breakfast, we walk wherever our legs take us. We spot a few guys from Portstown at the skating rink. I know them better than Mitch and Murray.

"Well, what do you reckon to this place?" I ask.

"It's friggin' brilliant, so it is….you couldn't beat it with a big stick….what do yous think yourselves?"

"Aye, it's good, the grub's good."

"We're self-catering, so we are…we heard that the food was cat."

I look to Mitch and Murray for support.

"No, it's dead on," says Murray.

Mitch seems to be in a quiet mood today. He's leaning over the railings, watching the skaters.

"Have yous tried the ice skating yet?"

Mitch looks around. "No, but we've tried the ice cream."

We all smile, and one of them pulls a face at Mitch.

"Who's the comedian, eh? We've got a comedian in our midst, boys."

It's a guy called Ambrose Flynn. He's one of those decent people who hang around with rascals and becomes one himself. When he talks, I listen earnestly, but I'm picturing a tin of Ambrosia creamed rice. He's here with the McGuire brothers. One brother is a dark six-footer, and the other is fair and five-foot-four. He looks like he won't sprout much further. His dark brother is an exception because most Portstown men don't get much beyond five and a half feet. Land of the Giants! We soon discover that size doesn't seem to matter. Seemingly the small brother pulled a bird last night and didn't get home until four o'clock in the mornin'. We're all ears.

"You should have seen her," cries Ambrose. "She was a

cracker...big blond, big tits...the whole shebang."

"You're havin' me on."

I want to tease more details from them. The older McGuire chips in.

"I don't know how the wee fucker does it...he'd get up on a cracked plate, so he would."

His face is animated, and I detect he's secretly ragin' because it wasn't him. I glance over at McGuire Junior. He's a friendly-looking culchie with pot-marked skin. It's not scabby or pimply like Free State people, but it's rough. His hair is wavy, and his shirt collar is too big for him. Maybe his ma shops in the same place as mine. He's no oil paintin', that's for sure.

"Did you do 'er?" Mitch has rejoined the conversation.

"Does a cat lick milk?" It's not McGuire but Ambrose speaking on his behalf.

"You're jokin'!"

McGuire laughs, and I'm convinced he's mocking the rest of us.

"Is the Pope a Catholic?" It's Ambrose again - the ventriloquist's dummy. I wish he'd shut his mouth and give his ass a chance. And I wish that McGuire would either confirm or deny it. Either he did, or he didn't! Instead, he returns to the ice rink with a big smirk glued to his face.

"He's been like that all mornin'," says his big brother. "But he definitely bucked her. Knowin' him, I'd say he was in and out of 'er like a Jack in the Box."

"Will we have a go at this ice skating crack, or will we just go back to the doughnut place?" I look over at Murray and Mitch. We all gurn at each other and then are on our way. The sun is trying to raise a gallop, and the Butlin's revellers are getting into full swing. I see a teenage couple in shorts, hand in hand, like they genuinely like each other. They're probably here for the whole week. No doubt they've been saving like crazy since last year for this holiday. As long as they have each other, they're content. They don't need to mix with anybody else. I'm sure they're

self-catering. No queuing, no checking the watch for teatime. Everything is done at their leisure! Happy days. Happy holidays! A middle-aged couple in front of us is inspecting a timetable. They're off to the ballroom dancing with the Redcoats. She's dressed up to the nines, and he's got Brylcreem on his hair. It's almost 11 a.m., but they'll arrive in time. A child is waddling down an alleyway, eating pink candyfloss. Her mother and aunt are twenty yards behind. The little girl's head is smaller than the candyfloss. She's wearing a pink dress, and I wonder if her mother purposely considered this before buying the treat. *It's probably just a coincidence, McCoubrey. No chance!*
We stop at a TV room that's full of people. Why come all the way to Butlins to watch the telly when you can do it at home for nothing? A women's 100 metres race is on. All, except one of the competitors, are black. The camera zooms in on the Jamaican runner.
"Jesus, wouldn't ye just love to ride the ass off that," shrieks Murray.
"Aye, but you'd have to catch her first," shouts Mitch.

After the doughnuts, we go to the Perspex pool. It takes us ten minutes to find the changing rooms. Nobody's singing "Yellow Submarine" today. Small clusters of friends and family are here to get exercise, to swim as many lengths as possible. Batten would love it. I'm headin' to the deep end, but I'm goin' to do breadths as it's my holidays, not the friggin' Olympic Games. I see a guy putting on his goggles. *He* won't be doing breadths. As we enter the pool, a big fat woman in a black swimsuit finishes another length. She looks at us with disdain.
This is my lane. Go and swim somewhere else!
Just for badness, I wait until she returns and step in at the same spot where she'll be turning. She sees me and stands up in the water five yards before the edge, quickly resuming in the opposite direction. I'm pretending that everything is entirely innocent, that I didn't mean to block her path or to ruin her rhythm. As if I would do a thing like that! Inside I'm pretty

delighted. It serves her right… stuck-up bitch! I can't stand people who think they own the place unless it's *me!* I'm sure she was about to do one of those fancy turns you see on "Grandstand". She can go home and swim in the bath if she wants a pool all for herself.

The three of us have an underwater race at Mitch's suggestion. The loser has to buy the other two doughnut rings. "Ready, steady… Murray is still shouting "go" as he dives in. Mitch has anticipated this, so I'm last to start. Murray's feet kick my face as I move forward, forcing me to surface for air. I bump into fatso again. She tut-tuts and swerves around me.

"We thought you had drowned there McCoubrey…I almost went back to look for you, but then I thought about the doughnut rings you're goin' to buy for us. Isn't that right, Mitch?"

"Yip, make sure mine's nice and fresh and sugary."

"I was trying to get past, but your friggin' legs were all over the place."

"Listen, don't be makin' excuses now. You finished last. No, in fact, you didn't even finish. By rights, you should get us an extra gravy ring each for not finishing."

I try to change the topic.

"Screw your man over there on the diving board…he thinks he's Tarzan…..with a bit of luck, he'll land on top of that bag who's swimmin' up and down."

"ME, TARZAN, YOU JANE," shouts Mitch. "AHAAAAAHAAAAAAH."

I turn to face the glass window because I don't like being embarrassed in public.

We're leaning back against the ledge at the deep end, resting. Murray breaks the silence with a fart and a comment. "Do yous remember last year when you two dirty blurts were kicked out of the pool in Portstown for having dirty feet…I'd almost forgotten about that?"

"But not quite, eh?" says Mitch.

"No, not quite...it just came to me there now."

He looks chuffed, and he's on a roll.

"I always wash my feet, whether I'm goin' to the pool or not."

"I thought that was the whole *purpose* of goin' to the pool," says Mitch. "A free wash and a swim at the same time. At least I don't piss in the water like some people...not lookin' at anyone in particular McCoubs."

"Oh, I see...let's gang up on McCoubrey here. First, he doesn't wash his feet; now, he pisses in the pool. Anything else boys, while you're at it?"

"Let's not go there," says Murray. It'll put me off my doughnuts."

I don't mind being slagged when I'm enjoyin' myself. Plus, I have to make allowances for the fact that Murray's da drove us here and will be drivin' us back. So I'll have to take Murray's slaggin' on the chin until we return home. I wonder if we'll stop off again for fish and chips. And if we do, would it be ignorant to expect his da to pay again? Not really. After all, he's a grown man, and I'm not a teenager yet.

We're at the disco. Every night is Friday night at Butlins, and if I had the man from Hewitt and Gills here, I'd be in paradise. I'm wearing a navy blue T-shirt and Wrangler jeans. I soon realise that I should have worn white. The disco lights illuminate anything white, making average-lookin' fellas look above average and average-lookin' girls seem beautiful. The music is louder and more modern than in the Variety Hall, though oddly enough, the hall itself isn't much bigger. I recognise a guy called Brian Gleeson. *He's* wearing white and has a silver earring. Good lookin', blonde hair, white T-shirt, pale blue eyes, denims with Doc Martens. He can't go wrong.

"Mitch, do you think I should run back to the cabin and change into something white?"

"What for?"

"Because white looks good on people in here."

"I wouldn't worry about it."

"Hmmmh...well you're wearing white, so you are."

"I put on the first thing I pulled out of the drawer, and anyway, sure all my T-shirts are white."

They're playing **T.Rex**. and the place is buzzin'. We find a space near the corner and sit to watch the talent. Other people look older than us, and I can hear plenty of Northern Irish accents. Four bouncers in black suits and bow-ties stand near the door. Three of them have a moustache. It must be a qualification for this line of work. I wonder if "Fresh Face" earns as much as the other three. I can see Gleeson jiving with a pretty girl in the middle of the dance floor. She's wearing a white cardigan. He's smirking, and she is smiling. She's really into it, and every time she jives, her big white teeth glisten in the dark.

"Screw yer man Gleeson, boys. Over there! He's friggin' elected, so he is."

"Maybe he's not," says Murray.

We stare in awe. I wish I was a few years older and could jive like that. **Load up, Load Up, Load Up, Ruuuberbullets.** They're playing my song. Groups of youths are ignoring the girls and dancing among themselves. It is a ploy to get attention from all and sundry; they sure have mine. These denim-clad Belfast boys aren't backward about going forward. They aren't afraid of being shown up like I would if I was dancing around like a latchico.

At the local hop, at the local county gaol.
Load up, Load up, Load up, Ruuuberbullets.

I'd be happy if they played this song all night. And if they want to play smoochy music, **Can't Live** by Harry Nillson. At the Variety Hall, they play **Jumblei Turkish pie filigumbo,** and I'm damned if I can make out the words or have the foggiest idea of the song. It's not a bad tune, mind you.

Something crashes to the floor. The thud is audible throughout the hall. I'm sure it's not a sound effect for a rubber bullet. Maybe a loudspeaker has toppled. More thuds. I see a frenzied mob of denim-clad youths lashing out at something. They form a chaotic circle. Screams and shouts bounce around the venue, and I glimpse Gleeson's white shirt smack in the middle of the melee. The lights have been switched on, but the music continues. **Load Up, Load up**... I spot the four musketeers rushing forward in Indian file and diving into the scrum. Boots and fists are flying. One guy strolls up from behind, pulling a studded black belt from his jeans. He jumps up and slams it on top of the head of one of the bouncers.

Half the people have fled, but some girls in jeans watch the action calmly as if it's no big deal. A few revellers are still dancing, and when the music stops, they stand with hands on hips, glaring at the DJ. Reinforcement bouncers arrive, along with two Redcoats who look like they couldn't beat snow off a rope. One of the Redcoats comes over and asks us to leave. "The Disco's finished for the night...c'mon lads, please leave quietly. Come on, folks. The show's over." Many of the Denim guys have dispersed. A small rump remains. Someone is lying in the middle of the floor. One of the Redcoats props him up. Blood is pouring from his nose, but I recognise the face. It's the bouncer without the moustache.

We spill outside and drift away. A few clusters remain nearby, but most have melted into the darkness. Like candyfloss! I hear shouts echoing through the accommodation block. Some guy runs around the corner, and I hear several large bangs.
"What was that?" cries Murray.
"They're smashin' the windows," says Mitch.
We reach the canteen. Its large curtains are flapping outside the windows, and a vast spread of glass is in smithereens on the ground. I look at the other boys.
"They've wrecked the friggin' place, so they have...it's unbelievable."
"Thoughtless fuckin' animals," says Murray. "What's goin' to happen about our breakfast in the mornin'?"
"Now you're talkin'," grunts Mitch.
We head back to the hut and discuss the situation.

"Those fuckers aren't going to spoil my night," says Murray. "What happened anyway?"

"It was one of the Belfast boys. He pinched a girl's ass, and the bloke she was dancin' with went haywire. The next thing I see is a big Doc Marten boot flyin' through the air and the pair of them getting stuck into each other, with the bouncers in the middle. The bouncers tried to kick the Belfast fella out, and he lost the bap... and then all their mates joined in."

"How do ye know about all this, Mitch?"

"Because I was lookin' at the girl's ass myself when it all kicked off."

We decide to try the adult disco since it's not too late. I wear my new jacket, shirt, and tie for good measure. We can wander into the ballroom venue quite easily. I buy white lemonade and crisps for the three of us, and we find a place in the corner. Looking around, we see that we're the youngest in the joint.

"This is a kip. Let's go."

It's Mitch.

"At least give it a half hour," I say, afraid that Murray will agree with Mitch. They start playing **Tie a Yellow Ribbon,** and the dance floor becomes packed with boyfriends, girlfriends, husbands, wives, men, women and grannies. I feel like an oddball observing this lot, but I'd rather be watching them than *be* one of them.

Tie a yellow ribbon round the old oak tree. It's been four long years. Do you still want me? Look at the cut of them! All sentimental and at ease with each other, mentally tying yellow ribbons for that special person! How flippin' boring is that? I wouldn't know where to find a yellow ribbon for a start. Once, I saw Lona wearing a thin *navy* ribbon, but that's the wrong colour. And even if I could find a yellow ribbon, I don't think I could find an *oak tree.* We've got a wooden table in our kitchen at home, but I don't think it's oak. I'm pretty sure it's Formica, just like the table in the Dundalk café. I could tie a ribbon around one of the blackberry bushes in our back garden, but that's hardly the same thing.

"Sure, let's give it another few minutes," I say. "There's Sylvia's Mother."
"Who's Sylvia?" says Murray and Mitch in unison.
"The *song,* you dimps… they're playing **Sylvia's Mother**.
Murray throws me a sarcastic look. He's not as soppy as me. He prefers Thin Lizzy or Van Morrison!

And the operator says 40 cents more
For the next three minutes
Please, Mrs Avery, I just gotta talk to her
I'll only keep her a while
Please, Mrs Avery, I just wanna tell her goodbye
I wallow in the sadness, mentally scrambling for the 40 cents to bid Sylvia farewell.
"This is your last McCoubrey…we'll hit the road after the next song."
Mitch says: "Aye," and gives me a pitying look. The song is "**Paper Roses**". Marie Osmond is the singer, and she has a lisp. There's something sexy about a girl singing Paper W*oses*, Paper W*oses*. I regret having to leave so soon and feel myself urging the song to last a bit longer. It doesn't disappoint…Paper W*oses*, Paper W*oses*. When it eventually finishes, Murray rises sharply and heads for the exit. Mitch looks at me and shrugs his shoulders. "Here… let's get out of here before I start enjoyin' it."

On the way out to the foyer, we pass two men who are dancin' with each other. Murray shakes his head from side to side and looks disgusted. "Screw those two," cries Mitch. "A pair of Free State Fruits….John Fitzpatrick and Patrick Fitzjohn." It takes a moment for the penny to drop. When it does, I splutter on the crisps I'm eatin' and almost choke. Little bits escape onto my chin, and I brush them back to my mouth with my index finger. Murray continues to shake his head. It's a relief for the three of us when we hit the cool night breeze and are first in the queue for the Hot Dog van.

"Would you prefer to be buried or cremated, McCoubrey?"
"I'd prefer to be back in that disco, so I would."
"Which would ye prefer?"
"I don't know."
Often I don't have an answer.
"What about you, Murray?"
"I'd prefer not to die instead."
"Wise up. I mean, if ye had to choose. It's a hypothetical question. I'd prefer to be buried, but I don't fancy being buried alive. Did any of yous see that film where the guy wakes up and discovers he's in a coffin? Imagine that happenin'."
"Jesus," I say, "I couldn't bear that...I think I'll ask to be buried standin' up. Although, come to think of it, maybe I *will* be cremated after all."
"I couldn't do that," shouts Crozier. "The thought of bein' burnt alive would kill me, so it would."

We're standing outside the canteen, and Murray's ma is rippin'.
"They've cancelled the bloody breakfast, and all because of a few drunken eejits from Belfast. You'd think they could've put us somewhere else for our breakfast. I mean, even if it's cold in there, so what? We can all wrap up and still have something to eat. It's the height of nonsense, so it is. What do you think, Jimmy?"
"You can say that again. I think they'll have to give us all a refund, that's what I think. If they can't lay on a bit of grub, there's not much point in us being here, is there? I see the Gardai have been called in. They're swarmin' all over the place, so they are."
Murray's ma continues.
"It's the height of nonsense. Whatever possessed them to start fightin' in the first place? I heard that they were even fightin' among themselves later on. Some woman from a couple of blocks away told me she heard a commotion and a racket at two

o'clock this morning like they were killin' each other. The whole atmosphere's been poisoned, and I'm not sure I want to be here anymore."

She faces us.

"What do yous think, boys? Do yous want to stay, or will we pack our stuff and go? We can stop off in Dundalk for our dinner because I could eat the hind legs off a donkey, so I could. And I can make a few sandwiches to keep us goin' until then."

"I don't care," says her son.

"Neither do I," says Mitch.

"And what about you, Barry-Joe?"

"I'll go with the majority...it's up to yourselves."

Murray's da butts in.

"Well here...there's no point in himmin' and haain'...we'll meet yous at the car in half an hour."

We pack up in ten minutes and then toss up to see who's going to buy the gravy ring doughnuts for old-time's sake. "Some you win and some you lose McCoubrey...don't be long...we're starvin'." Murray is lying on the bunk bed, smiling, and Mitch is brushing his teeth. It's a friggin' nuisance, but I lost the toss, so there's no way out. I buy seven fresh doughnut rings - two each and a sneaky one for me on the way back. The two fat ladies are in the queue and say "Good Morning" in unison. "I wish it were," I reply, as I stick half a warm doughnut into my gob. That's better! Bye-bye Butlins. See you later, alligator. In a while, crocodile! As I pass the see-through swimming pool, I start to make faces at one of the underwater swimmers. I ape her doing the breaststroke. "Yippie aye yay," I shout, "yippie aye yay." I don't give a shit about who might be listening. "So you can swim underwater...bully for you." I offer her a bite of my doughnut. She's not one bit amused. Two seconds later, the offer is withdrawn and deliberately pushed into its final resting place.

Bouncer Of Woodhouse Street

"What are you doin' back here so soon? I thought you were away until the weekend?"

"We left because of the riotin'. Did you not hear about it on the news?"

"I heard something but can't see how you were caught up in it. I thought I was goin' to get my head showered with you not being here for a week. Chance would be a fine thing."

"I brought you back some sticks of rock - green, white and yellow instead of the red ones. Where is everybody anyway?"

"It's Ben's birthday today, and lucky enough, Rory Rodgers across the road…it's his birthday too, and his ones are havin' a party for him, and they've invited Ben. Saves me the whole bother of it all."

"And the expense."

"That too…it's a whole palaver these days…birthdays. But sure, it's only a racket to get you to spend money that ye don't have."

"They have it to spend, and we don't."

"Don't you be cheeky, you cheeky git"

"Where's Lona?"

"She's away practising for the Irish dancing competition tomorrow."

"What, she's practising today or tomorrow?"

"She's practising today, and the festival is tomorrow…you may go and watch her in the competition since you've nothing better to do now you're home."

"Aren't you goin' to ask me what Butlins was like?"

"Well, I hope you enjoyed it because that's your gallivantin' over for the summer. "Did you wear the coat I bought ye?"

"Yeah."

"I hope you did after me goin' to all that trouble to get it for ye….make sure you hang it up before it gets ruined. I suppose you'll be expectin' your tea now you're back? Someday yous' uns are goin' to eat me out of the house and home, so yous are."

Getting some food has crossed my mind a few times since I arrived.

"Only if you're making somethin' for yourself...I'm not that hungry anyway."

I trudge upstairs to hang my jacket up. *Not that hungry McCoubrey? Pull the other one. There's bells on it!*

Now that I'm home, I wish I was back in Butlins. My room is a pigsty, courtesy of Ben. It's been waiting patiently for my return so that it can become ship shape again. It can wait a bit longer. Maybe I could try saying the magic word, and the room will become spick and span. I sit on the bed, cover my face and scrunch my eyes. I already feel like a silly idiot, but I've started, so I might as well finish.

Abracadabra!

A slow peep through my fingers reveals an Opal Fruits wrapper, a knitting needle, three odd socks, and a crumpled Irish News wrestling in the corner.

Abracadabra, Abracadee:

I uncover my face. No cigar!

I wish I was hoppin' on and off the toy train at Butlins or eatin' one of those succulent gravy ring doughnuts. Or swimmin' in the Perspex pool. A little game of pitch and putt would do nicely right now. I pull out one of several green, white and yellow rocks. Momentarily I feel Irish and patriotic. I start sucking but have no patience, so I try to bite it. *It* bites me. Eventually, I manage to free a chunk. The holiday will be well and truly over when I've eaten the rock. Maybe I can make it last for a day or so. I almost rupture my throat by swallowing a sharp piece. There'll be nothing left of this rock by the time Crossroads starts. *You know it, McCoubrey. Maybe you don't.*

The headline in the Portstown Times smacks me in the face.

DOG FOUND HANGED IN BROWNSVILLE.

I read it several times, trying to digest its meaning. I'm in no hurry to read the full report and am happy to stew on the headline. I look away from the newspaper in case I read any of the words; I want to maximise the thrill by picturing the scene first. It might have been an Alsatian, but they're big and scary, so I doubt it. Or a Poodle, but they're more like ornaments than pets. Poodles aren't allowed out of the house without being on a lead and wearing a Tartan blanket to keep them warm. I can't imagine it being a Greyhound, as they couldn't catch it. It must have been a mongrel. Portstown is full of stray mongrels. Who do I know in Brownsville that might be capable of hanging a dog? A few faces filter into my brain, including the fella that called me a *Fenian fucker* a few months ago. That evil bastard would hang the likes of *me* if he thought he would get away with it.

I'm savouring these thoughts, but something compels me to flick out of them and read the article. A passer-by discovered the dog when he was out for his daily morning walk at six am. It was entangled in barbed wire and hanging from a tree's branch. I wonder if it was an oak tree. Unfortunately, the dog was dead, and the shocked early morning walker raised the alarm. The police are looking for four youths spotted in the vicinity the previous evening. One is said to have "fuzzy" hair. The local police inspector described it as "a despicable act of savagery that words can't describe". He called those responsible "sheer animals".

"Have you read that about the people hangin' the dog?"
My ma looks up. "I was talkin' to Mrs Scullion from Brownsville up the town this mornin'. She knows the dog. It belongs to one of her neighbours. She said it was a scrawny mongrel that used to bark and bite people all the time and that it was better off dead."
"It's still not a very nice thing to do though, is it?"
"I suppose not," she replies. "Your tea's almost ready, so don't be

goin' out until you've had it."

After tea, I call round to Murray's house. I hear the toilet flushing, and his da walks into the sitting room, pulling up his trousers. He's wearing big white droopy Y fronts. "I didn't know you were there, Barry-Joe," he says, taking a redner. I pretend I haven't noticed, but we both know I have. Our uneasiness is soothed by Murray's ma offering to make tea. Harry McCoubrey appears on TV to read the news. Murray's da listens intently to the introductory headlines and follows his wife into the kitchen. I'm sure I can hear him washing his hands at the sink. Dirty blurt!

"I suppose your ma was surprised to see you home," says Mrs Murray.

"Aye, she was indeed."

"Ah, sure there wasn't much point in stayin' if it was all startin' to turn nasty. All it takes is a few idiots to spoil the holiday for everybody else. If I were there now, I'd just be getting ready to go out for a wee Babycham...isn't that right?"

"You're right enough there... and maybe more than one if I know you."

Murray stays silent. I've noticed that he doesn't say much in front of his parents. He puts me in an awkward position where I feel like I have to talk for the both of us and to be honest, sometimes I don't have much to say for *myself,* let alone him. I mean, they're *his* parents, not mine. Eventually, he says: "C'mon," and we go up to his bedroom to listen to a song called **Whiskey in the Jar** by THIN LIZZY. They've modernised this old traditional Irish song by using electric guitars instead of acoustic ones, and it's a brilliant version. After playing **Whisky in the Jar** ten times, Murray puts on a record called **Knockin' on Heaven's Door.** The song only has six words, and by the time he's played it five times, the Butlins' holiday is history. I can't listen to this friggin' thing any longer. "I'm away here," I say. When I'm outside and headin' home, I feel warm and happy. I'm singin' to myself. **"Knock Knock Knockin' on Heavens Door."**

It's nine o'clock in the morning, and Aunt Lizzie's in the kitchen drinking tea. Something's not right. She is smoking incessantly, and her cup shakes when she lifts it. My ma is paler than usual. When she sees me, she puts her index finger over her lip. It's to prevent me from talking, not her. I more or less stop breathing. If I can't breathe, there's no way I'll be able to speak. Lizzie looks up at me: "I suppose you wouldn't have heard." It's a statement. I look at my ma and see that I can resume breathing.

"What's wrong? I haven't heard anything."

"Ted's been lifted...this morning at six o'clock. The government has introduced internment and rounded up all the Catholics they think might be Republicans. I don't know why they came for our Ted...he was involved with the old IRA in the 1950s when he was single, but he's a fifty-year-old married man now with nine children, for God's sake. They weren't even goin' to let him change out of his pyjamas...only I reared up and called them all the names under the sun. I even made sure he got a few mouthfuls of tea into him before they took him away."

"Was it the police who came?"

"It was the police and the B Specials...they're a shower of bastards, the lot of them. There was a whole posse of the bastards and all to arrest a married man with a bad back. Sure, he couldn't even tie his own shoes, so they ended up taking him away in his slippers, so they did."

"When will he be let out?"

"God only knows," says my ma. "How long is a piece of string? Once they intern ye, they can keep you for as long as they deem fit, but hopefully they'll let Ted out sooner than that."

She beckons me. "Here Barry-Joe, run to the shop and get twenty Embassy Number 6 will ye, and be as quick as ye can. And make sure that man with one arm hands you the correct change."

When I return, Lizzie is drinking coffee and nibbling at a Paris bun, between chain-smoking. She blows the smoke out from the side of her mouth straight into the path of my kisser. I like the smell of cigarette smoke, but it's not my preferred breakfast choice. However, since her husband has just been interned, I'll have to put up with it.

"Any more news about Ted?" I ask.

My ma answers. "No, but they've lifted one of the Campbells, and before you ask, no, it's not the same Campbells as the one who stabbed that fella. It's different Campbells altogether. You wouldn't know them, so you wouldn't."

"Where do they live?"

"Here in Redville, but at the other end of the estate."

Lizzie stubs out her fag and chips in. "His da used to be a butcher up the town, but you wouldn't know him, son. You're too young."

I can't work out whether it's the butcher or the son I wouldn't know. By the look of things, it'll be better for all concerned if I don't know *any of them.* I'm too young and too small. I talk in my sleep and sleepwalk. I've got one pair of jeans and a coat and shirt that I'll grow into when I'm twenty-five. By Christ, this is cat!

Lona comes over when she sees me. "What are you doin' here…I thought you weren't comin'?"

"So did I, but your mother told me to keep an eye on you until she comes later on. She's with Lizzie Harbinson."

"I know. Mammy has already told me about Ted. She'll be here after dinner time."

Lona looks lovely in her Irish dancing costume. Its glistening embroidery is green, white and gold - the same colour as my Butlin's rock. She runs off with her friends, and I settle back in my chair. Watching the dancers on stage and listening to Irish music is strangely relaxing. I start giving the girls marks out of ten for their performance. 5 out of 10…didn't lift her legs high enough…7 out of 10…good balance and timing. Nice looking face and good legs as well.

Lona comes on stage, and I feel nervous. I hope she doesn't trip and show herself up in front of all these people. She doesn't disappoint, and I give her seven and a half out of ten. Just because she's my sister doesn't mean I can't give her better marks than the rest. She's the best so far and must have a medal chance. If she doesn't win a prize, there'll be a steward's enquiry.

She gets a commendation from the judges and is awarded third place. She brings her bronze medal over for me to admire. It rests serenely in a velvet box, the type you'd get if you bought a watch. "Barry-Joe, you promised me a rock if I won a medal, so I hope you're goin' to keep your promise."
She has her pretty friend with her, so I can't wriggle out of it. Not that I would have, because I'm secretly delighted with her success.
"I'll tell ye what…is this your friend?"
"Yes, it is, and her name's Alicia."
"Well, in that case, both of you can have a rock, one for yourself and one for Alicia. One each."
They look at each other and smile. Lona is clasping her precious bronze medal in her hand.
"If you see Mammy before me, pretend I didn't win anything. I want to see her face for myself when I tell her."
"Ok."
At that, the girls skip merrily away and become part of the general commotion.

I'm at the back of the hall, so slipping away quietly is easy. I can't abide those people who tell the whole world when they're about to go by coughing loudly or pretending they've lost something. They usually sit in the middle of the row, so they have to squeeze past other people, and they tend to be big and fat, with oversized heads. A man from Redville always insists on being the last one up for Holy Communion on Sundays. He walks up the aisle, and the congregation stares at him. He's got the most enormous head I've ever seen. Everybody calls him head and a half Haughey.

I dander away from the Town Hall towards the town centre. On my way, I pass the police station and a clothes shop with no customers. It's one of those places that people *stare* into but rarely enter. But, of course, if *somebody else* goes in there and proves that it is a shop, they might consider it. Someone taps me on the shoulder as he walks past. It's Mitch.

"What's the crack," he says. "Where are ye goin'?"

"I'm goin' round the bend, so I am. Do you want to come with me?"

"Wise up. Where are ye off to?"

"Nowhere in particular."

"I'm in a hurry McCoubrey. I've got a tip for one in the 2.15 at Newmarket. See you later. Have a look in the bettin' shop on your way home. If I'm there, I'm there; if I'm not, I'm not."

He scurries off, and I gaze at him. We only got back from Butlins yesterday, but the way he's acting, you'd think we hadn't gone. "You're some mate, Crozier," I mutter.

On the other side of the road, I spot Ambrose Flynn striding in dark trousers and a leather jacket. He clocks me and waves over enthusiastically. "That was some crack boy," he shouts across the traffic. His face is beaming, and his nose is as big as before. He will be one of those guys that latch onto you, wanting to be your friend. He'll say hello to me for the next ten years, just because I met him on holiday. He never said hello to me *before* I went to Butlins. So the next time I see him, I'll hide somewhere.

The town feels eerie today. Everyone seems to be in a hurry to go somewhere else. I bump into my ma and Ben on their way to the Irish Dancing festival.

"I thought you were in the Town Hall with Lona?"

"She's with all her wee friends. She's fine."

"How did she get on this mornin'?"

"She did all right."

"I suppose that means she didn't win anything, then?"

She looks disappointed.

"The results weren't in when I left…for all we know, she might have won a medal of some sort."

"There's nothing more about Ted. They won't tell Lizzie where they took him, and she's goin' up the wall. I've just heard that a whole lot were lifted down the Tunnel, too. So we'll just have to wait and see what happens. Some of the Protestant neighbours were gurning over at Lizzie and me this mornin' as if we were lepers. She told me they'd had nasty, threatening phone calls just after Ted was lifted, so somebody must have been in the know. The good news for her is that a friend of Ted who heard that he had been arrested, has offered the whole family a house in the Tunnel, and they might be flittin' next week. It's some man who's a Republican, on the run down in Dundalk, and has taken his family down South to join him, so his house is empty. So watch yourself when you're goin' home because there's a funny atmosphere around this place today."

"What's for tea?"

"If I'm not back in time, make yourself a banana sandwich," she says, as she walks off towards the shop with no customers.

I'm jolted by the knowledge that the Harbinsons might be flittin'. For now though, I need to suspend my reaction and focus on a necessary errand. My feet lead me to Woolworths without me telling them. I circle the biscuit counter and am irritated when I notice who is serving. It's Posh Girl's younger sister, who I've seen here a few times previously. She's far more impatient and snobbish than the older one. As she's plain and plump, she's not entitled to be like this. Feeling flush with my little leftover money from Butlins, I order whole fig rolls, custard creams, chocolate digestives, and a few pink wafers.

"That'll be fifteen new pence," she says curtly.

I observe that she's wearing hoop earrings, which aren't enough to elevate her from plain to sexy. Although I have the exact change, I give her a twenty new pence piece so that she can work for a living. When she's at the till, I peep into my white paper bag and notice that one of the chocolate digestives is broken. "One of these is broken," I tell her. She peers inside my bag and stares at me. Then, without a word, she removes the broken biscuit and replaces it with a whole one. Finally, she turns away, and when she faces me again, she is eating the digestive that I didn't want. "No wonder she's fat," I mouth to myself.

On my way home, I pass McGurty's newsagents. He sees me through the shop window and looks the other way. A few seconds later I recognise a man who knows my da. He's swaggering towards me from ten yards away, and I know he's going to say something.

"Alright, young McCoubrey ...how's your da?"

"Fine."

"Ye know everybody calls me the Bouncer of Woodhouse Street...any problems see me, young McCoubrey."

He toys with his belt.

"Have you seen that film, **A Fist Full of Dollars**?"

"Aye."

"Well, from now on, I'm the Clint Eastwood of Portstown."

He puts a big cigar into his mouth and eyeballs me.

"You see what I mean, young fella...there's no point unless you can walk the walk and talk the talk."

I start laughing to keep him happy.

"Yeah, I see what you mean, all right."

"This street ain't big enough for the both of us," he drawls.

He blows cigar smoke across my face. I must introduce him to Aunt Lizzie. He stares at me, hands on hips. A faint smile covers his face.

"Tell your da that the Bouncer of Woodhouse Street called him a baldy old bastard."

I get the message. "Alright," I say, grinning. Then I move on briskly in case I'm shot to pieces.

I want to sneak past Mitch, but he's outside the betting shop with Eddie Friel. He rubs his palms together when he sees me.

"Did it win?" I shout.

"Maybe it didn't!"

Eddie puts an arm on each of our shoulders.

"Come'ere, I've got a wee yarn to tell ye."

We huddle closer.

"I was in McKeever's pub last night, and I asked Francie for a Scotch on the Rocks. So he gives me a Scotch with water in it. So I pull him up on it." 'Here, Francie,' says I… 'I ordered a Scotch on the Rocks…this is water. So where's the ice?' "So he looks at me and shouts over: *'For frig sake, Eddie, what's the difference?'"*

A pause ensues, and Eddie looks like he's forgotten his punch line. Then, however, he returns to reality as suddenly as he had disappeared from it. He eyeballs Mitch and me in turn.

"Try tellin' that to the Captain of the Titanic," says I. "Try tellin' that to the Captain of the Titanic. He soon got the message, I can tell ye, and he didn't make the same mistake next time round."

Me and Crozier are in stitches. Crozier hands him a glistening silver coin.

"You're a flippin' scream, Friel…that's a good one, all right."

Eddie turns to me for approval. It *was* funny, but what does he want - a medal? Maybe I should go and fetch Lona's from the Town Hall.

I can't understand why no one has mentioned "Internment". From the doorway of the betting shop, I can see a few punters inside. They're engrossed in studying the form. A small group of women are having a whispered conversation across the road, but I can't very well go and earwig. So I decide to nip over to Granny McCoubrey's, as a cup of Rosy Lee is guaranteed. She's alone and has heard about Ted and the others.

"I'm sure you've heard about all the men being arrested…and it's not just here in Portstown…they've been lifted in Lurgan and Belfast as well…everywhere…God only knows where we're headed. Our Lizzie must be goin' up the wall. God, I hope and pray that she gets that house down here, the one she was tellin' me about earlier on."

I imagine our street without the Harbinsons. *Fewer of us to take on the Tartan Gang. Is this the first domino to fall for the Catholics of Redville? Could there be a mass exodus from our side, fleeing to the Tunnel or somewhere else that's safer?*

I sense myself shuddering. With fear!

Suddenly my granny starts laughing.

"Have you heard about that fella Minksy Molloy, who lives a few doors away? He stole a pig from Dennys the other day and keeps it in the bathroom - in the bath itself. I couldn't get over it when I heard about it, so I said to him yesterday when he was walkin' past the house: 'Minksy, what about the smell?' 'Oh,' he said, 'the pig will just have to get used to it.'" We both start laughin', and she doesn't stop until her eyes are moist.

"Did you ever hear the likes of that in your life?"

It's great to see her happy, even for five minutes.

Up Goes The Flag

I'm walking through Redville on my way home. I spot Pope chatting to a group of Denim-clad fellas. All Protestants! I wave. He nods and acknowledges me with his index finger. I thought for a second that he was about to use *two* fingers. He looks pale and stern. I look back and sense that the other boys are asking Pope about me. It agitates me. I don't want those effers talking about me behind my back. None of them!

A wooden stick with a square piece of ragged black nylon attached is hanging out of Harbinson's upstairs window. Jesus Christ! I don't believe it. It must be a protest against internment. *How come my ma didn't mention it down the town earlier?* I can't stop lookin' at the black flag, and a ripple of nervous energy attacks my body. The horn sounds for the end of today's shift, and the Ulster Laces workers file homeward. They are dreaming of an Ulster Fry, followed by Crossroads. Some notice the black flag and point at Harbinson's house. A few look around to chastise the neighbours for tolerating the situation. One matronly worker folds her arms in disgust and stands facing Harbinson's house, staring at the flag as if expecting a response. The front door opens, and one of Lizzie's sons eyeballs the factory worker. He folds his arms precisely like her. She shakes her head and shuffles off. A few paces later, she looks around and is met by Harbinson's piercing eyes, escorting her to the bottom of the street. He goes back inside, closing the door with a deliberate bang that echoes through the street.

I hear on the radio that some internees have commenced a hunger strike, protesting their detention. The thought of someone doing without food and maybe starvin' to death makes me shudder. Surely it would be better and more enjoyable to *eat* yourself to death. Twenty-seven stones in weight. Another Mars bar and a packet of crisps, and you're a goner! What a way to say cheerio to the world. I scold myself for trivialising what I know is a serious issue. *A Wagon Wheel from death? No, McCoubrey, stop it now...no more talk about chocolate or sweets. Don't be jumpin' on the bandwagon.* I smirk at my little pun and know I'll soon tell the boys about the McCoubrey alternative to the hunger strikes.

Through the sitting room window, I see the nylon flag is still flyin' high. I'm glad. In the distance, I see my ma, Lona and Ben. My ma is carrying a shopping bag. I wait until she passes Harbinson's house, giving it a cursory glance, and I detect quiet satisfaction on her pretty face. *She knew fine rightly about the flag!* Ben is holding her hand, and Lona hovers at her side, inspecting something every few moments. My mother is walking in a deliberate and upright way. I rush into the kitchen and put the teapot on. I'll have a nice cup of tea ready by the time she takes her coat off. Perched on the window sill, I see a box of **OMO** soap powder. I stare mockingly at the three big white letters.
"On my own, eh?"
I'm aware that I'm talking out loud.
"Somehow, I don't think so!"

I'm upstairs, flicking through my ma's records. I play **From a Jack to a King** about twenty times. I try singing: *From a Jack to a King,* but the harder I try, the squeakier my voice becomes. *Best leave it to Elvis, McCoubrey.* My da's favourite is next, Charlie Pride's **Crystal Chandeliers.**
Oh, the crystal chandeliers light up the paintings on the wall, The marble statuettes are still standing in the hall...
Tears peep out of my eyes. When I hear more of Charlie, they fall to my cheekbones. I let them be. Nothing makes me happier than to be sad. Time for more happiness! Playing **Massachusetts** at the end is like eating the meat last. I savour the haunting singing of Robin Gibb. He was recently on Top of the Pops, dressed in black, head to toe! Dangling on every word, I hope that it never ends. But it does. It's a short song, less than three minutes. All

you need for a hit these days is a catchy sentence, and you're elected. Then just as the lights are going down in Massachusetts, I hear raised voices downstairs.

"What's goin' on?" I enquire.
"Somebody stole money from Mammy's purse, and it wasn't me, so it wasn't." Lona looks eager to find the culprit.
"That only leaves yous two," says my ma, eyeing me. "Was it you?"
"Nope."
"Ben, you're in for it. It *was* you, ye wee skitter, wasn't it?"
"I haven't seen your money. I haven't even seen your purse, so I haven't."
I want this resolved, especially as it wasn't me. So I turn to Ben.
"Empty your pockets, sunshine."
He obliges.
"See, nothin'. Sickened, aren't ye? I'm always gettin' the blame. You can even search in my socks if ye want."
"One of yous is a thief and a liar," shouts Ma. "I'm sick to the back teeth of openin' my purse and findin' that there's money missin'."
"What's for tea," roars Ben.
"I haven't bloody decided yet."
I haven't finished my inquisition.
"Hi boy…I think I will just have a look in your socks."
He kicks his shoes off and lifts his feet one at a time.
"See, nothin' there."
"The socks."
He reddens and takes one sock off.
"The other one."
He hesitates.
"What've ye got to hide?"
It's my ma, standin' over him.
"It's him, all right," I yell. Tell him to take the other one off."
"Take it off, Ben, this bloody minute."

He obeys and exposes a bare foot. I pick the sock up, and it's lumpy. So I turn it upside down. Two shiny silver decimal coins sink to the floor and dance on the oilcloth for a few seconds before resting.

"I found it on the floor. What about Finders Keepers, Losers Weepers?"

"You'll be weepin' in a minute, so ye will"

She slaps his face.

"That's for stealin'."

"I was goin' to give it back, so I was."

She gives him a harder smack.

"And that's for tellin' lies."

His cheeks are stinging, but he doesn't react. Instead, he turns around and resumes watching Popeye, hastily putting his socks back on.

I ask her to buy me a new school blazer.

"What's wrong with the one you've got?"

"I don't like wearin' second-hand things."

"If you don't wear the uniform, you'll be suspended by the Head." I throw her a startled look.

"Of the school, I mean. What did you think I meant?"

"Nothin'… that blazer almost got me killed a few months ago in Belfast."

"Your new school's not in Belfast…it's a ten-minute walk from the house, so it is."

"So that's that then?"

"It is indeed, yes."

I peer out of the sitting room window. It's bucketing. Walter McGee walks past. He lives on the edge of Redville in a house with a thatched roof. I see another man being followed by a posse of dogs. His hair is ginger, *and* he's going bald. He probably still lives with his ma. It's lucky for him that he likes animals. Pope comes into view. Denim-clad, hands in pockets. In a world of his own! I wonder if he still has the scarf. He knows where he can stick it. Good riddance to bad rubbish. Sharon Hobsbawn's face is pressed against her front window. It looks like she's there for the duration. She doesn't look away when our eyes meet. Mmmhh!

I hear the back door open and close. "Woust for a wee second," cries my da. He's in the gypsy chair, holding his cap. His black donkey jacket fills the seat. My ma's dainty hands are resting on his shoulders. Lona and Ben are at the table. Banana sandwiches! Hetty's must be back in business. Suddenly I hear a familiar voice, and a rush of sickly adrenalin flows through my body. I swivel round to face our new colour TV. There he is, the man himself. I wonder what he's got in store for us tonight.

* * *

Printed in Great Britain
by Amazon